RUNNING CROOKED

Despite his innocence, Taw Landry served five years in prison for robbery. Freed at last, his troubles seemed over, but when he reached the home range, they were just beginning. He was determined to discover who'd stolen twenty thousand dollars from the stage office in Cottonwood. But Taw's resolution was overtaken by events. Murder was committed and rustling was rife as Taw tried to unravel the five-year-old mystery. As the guns began to blaze — could he survive to the final showdown?

Books by Corba Sunman
in the Linford Western Library:

CORBA SUNMAN

RUNNING CROOKED

Complete and Unabridged

LINFORD
Leicester

First published in Great Britain in 2007 by
Robert Hale Limited
London

First Linford Edition
published 2009
by arrangement with
Robert Hale Limited
London

British Library CIP Data

Sunman, Corba
    Running crooked.—Large print ed.—
Linford western library
1. Western stories
2. Large type books
I. Title
823.9'14 [F]

ISBN 978–1–84782–549–0

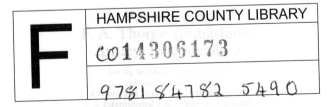
This book is printed on acid-free paper

1

The trail skirted a mesa which reared up into the bright sky in sharp, rocky escarpments before descending to a lower level of ground which formed the last stretch of the ride to the huddled collection of buildings called Cottonwood. A stiff breeze blew red dust into swirling dust devils as Taw Landry halted his gaunt buckskin on a sandy knoll and gazed across the semi-desert at the little community in west Texas. He twisted in his saddle and gazed over his broad shoulder at the seemingly deserted back trail, pulling the brim of his Stetson a fraction lower to shade his blue eyes, and his narrowed gaze studied the distant features of the wasteland.

Nothing moved back there but he continued to watch for movement, although he had taken pains to avoid other men since getting out of prison two weeks before — spurning all human contact as he adjusted his mind from convict to free man. Now he was back on home range, keenly aware that an accounting was to be had for a crime he did not commit. The desire to exact payment from the real culprit for his five years in jail was a bright flame in his heart which nothing but final settlement could quench.

The horse shifted its weight and nodded its head. Landry faced his front and kneed the animal into motion. For five long years he had ached to return to the DL ranch owned by his father, Dave Landry, but now, facing the last short stretch, he felt strangely reluctant to traverse it, for stark reality lay ahead and he had no idea who had robbed the stage office in town and framed him with the crime.

The sun was close to the western skyline as he continued, crossing rangeland now: sparse clumps of grass which would sustain nothing but longhorn cattle in this south-west area of Texas. The lowering rays of the sun were reflecting from the tops of a distant mountain range, throwing crimson talons of natural fire across the sky and long blue shadows which crept stealthily across the undulating ground in all directions.

Darkness came suddenly, but Landry knew this country intimately, the preceding five years slipping away as if they had never existed. He continued at a steady lope towards the cluster of lamps now marking Cottonwood. A thin yellow splinter of the moon showed in the east and stars appeared like diamonds in the velvet cobalt sky. The torturous breeze which had caused him to sweat through the long hours of daylight now lost its fierceness and cooled to a tolerable degree.

Landry reined in at the end of the main street and sat his mount while his gaze sought out the well-remembered lay-out of the town. He recalled his last time here, when he had been chained and carted off to prison to begin his sentence. Nothing seemed to have changed during his absence, and he didn't doubt that life had gone on as if nothing had happened, except to him. He had spent five years in purgatory, and felt a leaping urge in his breast at the thought of finally getting to grips with the crooked plot which had resulted in his incarceration.

He rode along the street to the livery barn, his keen blue eyes missing nothing of his surroundings. Tall in the saddle, his big frame had filled out and become work-toughened by the hard labour he had done in prison. His height was two inches over six feet, and swinging a sixteen-pound sledgehammer for countless hours day after endless day had hardened him into superb physical fitness. His muscular body had become inured to the terrible regime he had experienced behind bars and his lean features carried eloquent marks of his suffering.

A man stepped into the lighted

doorway of the barn from the interior and paused in mid-stride when Taw swung down from his saddle. He recognized the man instantly but gave no sign of recognition.

'Howdy. I'm Bill Tarleton and I'm on my way to supper,' the ostler said. 'You've caught me on the hop. I'm in a hurry. Are you staying long in town?'

'I expect so.' Taw kept his face in the shadows as he reached into his pocket and produced a silver dollar, which he flipped into Tarleton's ready hand. 'Let me know when you want some more.'

'Sure thing. Use any empty stall. See you later.'

Tarleton stepped around Taw and went on his way. Taw led the buckskin into the barn and took care of its needs. Then he paused to consider. His desire was to ride to DL and see his father, but he was aware that the old man had taken the situation of his son's apparent lapse into crime in less than kindly fashion and had apparently disowned him, as had Sadie Grimmer, the girl he

5

had once expected to marry. There had been no communication from Landry senior during the five years Taw had spent in jail. He had written twice, but ceased his overtures when not one word of reply came from the older man. Sadie had written once, but only to tell him that her father had ordered her not to have anything more to do with a convicted criminal.

Taw took his rifle and blanket roll and then paused, for an intangible trickle of foreboding made its presence felt in his chest. A slight rustling sound had come from the dense shadows outside the circle of radiance thrown down from the overhead lamp, causing him to reach for the butt of his pistol. A horse stamped and then there was complete silence, but he sensed that someone was waiting in the stable and tensed his muscles, expecting a shot out of the dark. When nothing happened he departed quickly, intending to rent a room at the hotel along the street.

Keeping to the dense shadows on the

street, he walked slowly, his mind back there in the past, recalling the bitter moments of his arrest and subsequent trial. Everyone had believed him guilty of robbery, but he was keenly aware that someone knew he was innocent — the unknown man who had robbed the Wells Fargo stage office — and he had no idea who that could be. But he would find out. He would spare no effort to locate the guilty man and clear his name.

The town was fairly quiet. A guitar was being strummed in a saloon, the music sounding strangely muted in the darkness. Carrying the rifle in his left hand, Landry brushed the fingers of his right hand against the butt of the .45 Colt Peacemaker riding in the scuffed holster on his thigh. Again he was suddenly wary, his senses alerted by a faint unnatural sound that emanated from an alley mouth as he passed by.

Taw did not break his stride but stepped aside and twisted around to face the alley. He heard a boot scuff hard ground in the impenetrable darkness, and then a low-pitched man's voice called vibrantly.

'Is that you, Taw Landry?'

Taw dropped to one knee, easing his pistol from its holster as he did so. His mind was filled with question. No one could possibly know he was back from prison. He did not reply and silence stretched through the hostile shadows.

'Landry, declare yourself.' The voice was tense. 'I'm a friend, and I want to warn you that the dice are loaded against you. They've got the town staked out for you, and this time you won't be railroaded into prison; now they plan to kill you.'

'Give me a name,' Taw rapped. 'Who are you talking about? I'm Taw Landry, and I just got into town. How in hell did you know I had returned?'

Red flame spurted in answer from the shadows just along the street and the crash of a shot blasted the silence. A slug cracked past Taw's right ear; would have hit him dead centre if he had not been down on one knee. He blinked against the flash but refrained from replying to the shot and waited for the echoes to fade. When silence returned he arose and inched into the mouth of the alley.

The shot had been fired at him from a doorway on the street a dozen yards away, and the man who had spoken to him from the alley had departed before the echoes faded. Taw awaited developments, but nothing stirred around him and he holstered his pistol. He was about to move on when boots sounded on hard ground and he caught a glimpse of a figure coming towards him along the sidewalk.

'You there,' a voice called harshly. 'Stand still and put your hands up. Who fired that shot?'

Taw stepped further back into the alley, turned, and ran for the back lots. He reached the end of the alley, dived sideways to the left, and had barely found the cover of the rear of the building at his side before a six-gun blasted from the street-end and slugs crackled through the night. Taw moved away instantly. He ran along the rear of the buildings fronting the street before turning into another alley and making for the street. As he reached the alley mouth some fifty yards from the spot where the first shot had been fired, a man stepped out of the shadows and stuck the muzzle of a pistol into his ribs.

'Hold it. Who in hell are you? Why are you prowling around in the dark?'

Taw acted instinctively, pushing away the muzzle of the gun as if swatting a fly and sledging his right fist against the man's jaw. The man cried out and went down to land inert on the ground. Taw bent, snatched up the discarded pistol, and hurled it away into the darkness. As he straightened, another man called from just along the street.

'What's going on? Have you got him, Barney?'

Landry scooted back into the alley and cannoned into a slight figure that was invisible in the dense shadows. He overbalanced and fell in a sprawl, knocking the figure to the ground in his headlong fall. He heard a smothered cry of pain. His hands grasped at the newcomer and he quickly realized that he had collided with a female.

'What are you doing out here?' he demanded, getting to his feet. He helped the girl up, aware that whoever was out to get him must be closing in right now.

'I'm on my way to visit a sick woman,' came the muffled reply. 'I'm Brenda Elwood, the doctor's daughter. You're Taw Landry, aren't you?'

'It seems everyone in town knows I'm back,' he remarked.

'Come with me quickly.' She grasped his arm and hurried deeper into the darkness of the alley.

Taw went along with her. After a few yards she stopped and opened an alley door. They entered a house and she closed the door and thrust home a bolt on the inside. A lamp was burning in a long passage, and Taw looked down into the girl's upturned face.

'I can see you're Taw,' she observed. 'You've changed in the past five years, but I would have recognized you. So you're back at last, and they've got the town covered to nail you.'

'Who are they?' he demanded.

She had a sensitive face, finely boned and framed in golden curls. Her blue eyes were wide as she gazed at him. Landry saw that she was wearing a blue silk dress that did not conceal the slender lines of her tall figure. There was a vivacious look about her that drew his attention like a magnet attracting metal, and he caught his breath as his senses recorded her appearance.

'You've changed some over the past five years,' he observed. 'I remember you as a skinny schoolgirl who couldn't keep her lip buttoned. You were full of sass, too.'

'Thank you for the compliment.' She laughed showing perfectly even teeth and her whole countenance was transformed into radiance. 'A girl needed a sharp tongue with males like you around.' Her smile faded and a frown appeared between her finely arched brows. 'You've come back to a load of trouble, Taw,' she observed in a harsher tone. 'The town has some wild dogs who want to pull you down.'

'I thought my troubles were over when I got out of prison,' he observed. 'But it seems they're only just beginning. How did news of my release arrive here before I did?'

'That's easy to explain. The prison people notified Sheriff Whitney of your release date.'

'Ah!' Taw nodded. 'So that's it. They've stacked the game against me, huh?'

'For what it's worth, I believe you are innocent of robbing the stage office, and a number of folks around town have the same opinion. But there's a faction operating outside the law, and it seems that they plan to use your return to further their crooked plans.'

'How do you know that?' Taw's gaze was almost devouring her face.

'I work as Doc's nurse, and I get to talk to all the sick people around town. I hear the rumours making the rounds. People trust me because I devote my life to helping them, and they tell me things they wouldn't dream of mentioning to anyone else. You're in a lot of trouble, Taw. Brad Cadell showed up in town just after you went to prison, and in five years he's bought himself a big share of local business. This town belongs to him now, and he's ruthless. He employs a number of bully boys to look after his interests. He bought out several small ranchers, and I'm sure he's behind the trouble your father is getting right now, which has steadily increased over the last few months.'

'There's trouble at the DL?' Taw's eyes narrowed and his expression hardened. 'Is my pa OK?'

'He's been ill. The last time he was in town someone caught him in a dark corner and beat him unmercifully. I nursed him and he's much better now, but the spirit seems to have gone out of him. He told me he was hanging on out there until you came back to take over.'

'He said that?' Taw frowned and shook his head. 'He cut me off without a word when I went to prison. I last saw him the day they took me away, and he was against me then. I wrote him a couple of times but got no reply, and figured he had turned his back on me.'

'Well, he's been counting the days to your release, and you'd better get out to DL as soon as you can and talk to him.'

A rough hand grasped the handle of the alley door and shook it violently.

'He didn't go in here,' someone said harshly. 'He's high-tailed it. I reckon he's halfway to the DL ranch by now.'

'Keep searching the town,' another said. 'He'll stick around until he's got the drift of how things are around here. We need to nail him pronto.'

Taw stood looking into Brenda's taut features until they heard receding footsteps in the alley. When the men outside had departed he moved restlessly, and Brenda caught hold of his arm as he eased towards the door.

'You can't go out there, Taw,' she protested. 'They'll shoot you down like a mad dog. You'd do better to stay in here until dawn and then make a run for it.'

'I don't feel like hiding or running,' he replied, his face hardening into a mask.

'I've never thought of you as a fool,' she retorted, 'and only a lame brain would go out now with the whole town up in arms. Someone must have paid a lot of money to get the townsmen up on their hind legs and baying like a pack of hound dogs. If you want to beat this you've got to be smarter than they are.'

Taw stood while a battle raged in his brain. Sweat beaded his forehead, but he saw the wisdom in her words and made an effort to accept the situation. He relaxed slowly and nodded.

'Thanks for the advice, Brenda,' he

said. 'I'll do like you say. I'll stay here until just before dawn.'

'That's better.' She smiled. 'I have to see a patient now. Doc won't be home tonight. He's out at Bill Temple's ranch. Mrs Temple is in labour. Make yourself comfortable. I'll be back in about an hour, and then I'll prepare supper. Shoot the bolt on this door when I leave, and I'll knock when I return.'

Taw agreed and Brenda departed. He bolted the door and went along the passage to a sitting room. His thoughts were in turmoil, and hiding away did not help him at all. He needed to be out there learning what he could, but was aware that a wrong move would kill him.

His patience fled in the face of the problems that seemed to be stacking up against him. He paced the room, his hands clenched. How could he fight such a set-up? It would not help to seek aid from the law, for it was obvious that the local law was involved. With efficient law dealers, the wrongdoing would have been stamped out as soon as it reared its head. He smiled cynically. He had been framed with a robbery, and they had wasted no time in getting rid of him. But why had he been singled out? Admittedly, he had been a hell-raiser in his youth, but he had never broken the law. Had the bad men seen him as a threat to their progress when they began to operate?

His anger flared when he thought of his father, and he knew he had to get out to the DL ranch as soon as possible. He paced the room, considering the situation, and was beside himself with impatience when he heard a knock at the alley door. Every instinct was protesting at inactivity as he went in answer, and he half-drew his pistol as he opened the door.

Brenda bustled into the house, and she seemed to be bursting with news. Her eyes were wide, her breathing ragged as if she had been running. Taw tensed, sensing that she was the bearer of bad news.

'You'll never guess what's happened,

Taw,' she gasped. 'Sadie Grimmer has been found murdered in her cabin and the sheriff is looking for you. They're saying you've killed your ex-girlfriend because she left you when you went to prison. Someone reported hearing angry voices at her place, before there was a scream and then a sudden silence.'

Landry was shocked by the news. He gazed at Brenda while his brain raced to get a grip on the situation.

'They've got you in a corner,' Brenda said. 'Right now you'll be blamed for everything that happens around here. Someone is calling the shots, and they're all directed at you. How can you defend yourself against these accusations? There's even talk of a lynching when you are caught.'

'When was Sadie killed?' he asked.

'She was seen in the general store at about four-thirty this afternoon. Nobody saw her after she left. A witness said it was just after eight when Sadie screamed in her cabin.'

'Didn't the witness see anyone leave

her cabin after the scream?'

'I didn't hear. All the talk is about getting you and putting a rope around your neck.'

'How was Sadie killed?' Taw's memory was thrusting up images of the girl as he had seen her last, crying on the street because he was on his way to jail.

'She was struck on the head with something like a gun butt. That's what the sheriff thinks. He's got all the able-bodied men in town out there searching for you, Taw. They think the killer will have blood on his clothes. You've been sighted all over town, even though you've been shut up in here.'

'Someone wants me out of the way mighty badly.' Taw shook his head. 'I've got to get out of here, Brenda.'

'I think your best bet is to remain until they stop searching for you. If you're taken they'll lynch you. Nothing you could say would help you. Everyone is certain you've come back to cause trouble. You've been judged and found guilty, and you can expect no mercy in Cottonwood. Someone is using you to further his own crooked ends, and it looks like he is succeeding.'

Landry gazed at the girl while his mind raced with conjecture.

'I didn't reach town until about eight this evening,' he said thoughtfully. 'I rode straight to the livery barn, and Bill Tarleton was leaving to get his supper. I gave him a dollar. He'll remember the time, so I should have an alibi.'

'What makes you think Tarleton will be on your side when the rest of the townsfolk are against you?' Brenda countered.

Landry exhaled in a deep sigh. His pale eyes glittered as he tried to find a safe way out of the maze of events encompassing him. As he dropped a hand to his gun butt a heavy knock sounded at the alley door. Brenda froze, her face expressing fear. She reached out trembling fingers, grasped Landry's arm in a restraining movement and shook her head warningly when he glanced at her.

'This is the doc's place,' a voice said loudly in the alley. 'He's out at the Temple place tonight. Miz Temple's time has come. Brenda is always out, visiting the sick. We'll have to come back later.'

Footsteps receded and Taw breathed easier.

'I'm leaving, Brenda,' he said firmly. 'I'll try and get the sheriff on his own and talk to him. If I run I'll never be able to prove my innocence.'

'If you confront the sheriff he'll put you behind bars, and you'll never get the chance to prove your innocence,' she retorted.

'That's a chance I'll have to take. Thanks for your help. I appreciate it.'

'If you're set on a showdown then I'll try and get the sheriff to come here. You can't show yourself on the street, Taw. They'll shoot you on sight.'

'I don't want you to get mixed up in this.' He shook his head. 'I'll do it my way, and if anything goes wrong I'll only have myself to blame. Can I leave my rifle and saddle-bags here? They're in your sitting-room.'

'It'll be your funeral.' Brenda shrugged, aware that he had made a decision and could not be swayed from it. 'I'll take care of your things.'

Taw patted her shoulder and went to the alley door. He slid back the bolt and eased the door open a couple of inches. The alley was black. He listened intently but heard nothing beyond the sighing of the wind rushing along the alley. He drew a deep breath, restrained it, and went outside quickly, closing the door noiselessly at his back. This was the point of no return, and he had no way of knowing how it would end. He had to start fighting the situation confronting him, and this was the only way he could do it.

He reached the alley mouth, and bumped into two men who were standing just around the corner. A pistol muzzle was thrust hard against his stomach and rough hands grasped him. His pent-up anger exploded in his mind, fed by the injustice of the situation, and he whirled into action with the ferocity of a female cougar protecting her cubs, his impatience at an end and his determination flaring.

2

Taw drove his right fist into the shadowed face that loomed before him while his left hand flashed out to turn away the deadly gun muzzle prodding his stomach. His knuckles cracked against a solid chin and there was a cry of shock and pain as the man spun away under the force of the blow. His clawing fingers closed around the second man's gun wrist and he twisted it viciously as he flung his body sideways away from the gun. The weapon exploded raucously, and he heard the bullet crackle skywards. He struck again with his right fist and felt the man's nose crumple under his hard knuckles. He wrenched the pistol from the man's hand.

Both men were down. Taw paused for a moment before turning and running into the alley. He headed for the back lots, carrying the gun he had taken from his assailants, and heard the commotion raised by the men as he stepped into cover at the rear of the doctor's house. He regained his breath and went to the right, intent on talking to the sheriff. He had to stay on the right side of the law.

He reached the rear of the jail and paused in the dense shadows, listening intently. The silence seemed to mock him. He thought of his father and raw anger spilled through him. It was time he discovered who was causing the trouble in this county and did something about it.

The street end of the alley beside the jail was deserted. Landry paused in the shadows and looked around. He could hear a commotion going on along the street where he had bumped into the two men. A light showed in the law office window fronting the street. He stepped out of the alley and sidled towards the window. A quick glance through the glass showed him the interior of the well-remembered office, and he recognized the big man seated at the desk towards the rear of the long room. Sheriff Whitney was on duty, and alone.

Taw opened the street door and stepped into the office. He was holding the spare pistol down at his side, and paused to thrust it into his waistband. His eyes narrowed as he regarded Sheriff Ben Whitney. The county lawman was a solid-looking man past forty, with wide shoulders and a bulky body which was more muscle than fat. His round face had a wide forehead, from under which his brown eyes peered suspiciously at the world. A thin-lipped mouth looked as if it had been slashed with a skinning-knife, and his long, broad nose had been broken in his youth and had healed crookedly, bent slightly to the right. His cream Stetson was pushed back off his forehead, and a straggle of brownish hair curled forward untidily.

'Taw Landry.' A shadow crossed

Whitney's face as he leaned back in his seat. 'Long time no see! So you got your debt to the community paid off, huh? Now you're back to resume your life.' He shook his head. 'But it ain't gonna be that easy, Taw. Trouble was brewing in the county when you went away, and you've come back to find it on the boil.'

'I didn't kill Sadie Grimmer,' Landry said sharply.

Whitney nodded. 'I wouldn't expect you to come in here and confess to her murder,' he said. 'But on the face of it you're saddled with it. Take a peek at the facts. Sadie left you five years ago because you went to jail, and she was killed soon as you got back. You got to admit that looks mighty suspicious, huh?'

'From where I'm standing it's obvious someone used Sadie as a means to saddle me with murder.'

'You got any idea who would do a thing like that?'

'The same man who railroaded me to

prison five years ago with the stage office robbery. I've got no idea yet who did that, but I mean to find out.' Taw paused and gazed at the sheriff as if hoping he might come up with an answer to the mystery.

The sheriff grimaced and shook his head. 'That could prove to be difficult. I checked around the county at the time and found there was a watertight case against you, and it still looks like you did it. Now you're back, and someone has got the townsfolk riled up over you. Most of them are out there on the street right now, looking for you. There's talk of a lynching if they lay hands on you. I've spoken to them but they ain't in the mind to listen to me.'

'I know. I bumped into a couple of them.'

'And they couldn't hold you.' Whitney nodded. 'That's no more than I would expect, knowing you for the hell-raiser you used to be. Did you kill anyone in getting away?'

'No.'

'That's good. It's lucky for you Bill Tarleton saw you when you arrived in town. He put the time at some minutes after witnesses said they heard Sadie screaming in her cabin, so unless you were able to be in two places at once then I'm satisfied you didn't kill her. As far as I'm concerned, you got no charge to answer.'

'So what's with all the talk about me getting lynched?'

'It won't happen. That's just talk. Those men out there will all head back into the saloon shortly and fill up on the drinks that are being offered free.'

'Who's behind this? Do you know?'

'Sure, I know. But I can't prove it. I'm waiting and watching, and soon as I get proof I'll act on it. You know the way the law works.'

'And what do I do in the meantime? I need to get out to the DL. I heard my pa was beaten up. I'm entitled to protection from the law.'

'Yeah. I been giving that a lot of thought since I learned you was on your way back from jail. It may surprise you to know that I never believed you guilty of robbing the stage office, Taw. But all the evidence pointed so neatly to you. It was surprising, the men who came forward five years ago to say they saw you acting suspiciously on the night of the robbery. I've spent the last five years trying to unravel events, but so far I've had no luck. All I do know is that now you're back things will begin to hum, and you're gonna be right in the thick of it.'

'Didn't any of the stolen money show up after I was jailed? Twenty thousand dollars went missing from the stage office, so what happened to it?'

'It didn't show, apart from that wad I found in your father's barn, and folks are saying it won't see daylight until you get back and start spending it.'

Taw shook his head impatiently. 'Someone did a pretty neat job of framing me, huh? So what happens now? I can't walk out of here without running the risk of getting lynched.

How in hell can I hunt around for the man who railroaded me into prison?'

'There's only one way you can beat this set-up.' Whitney opened a drawer in his desk and rummaged inside. He produced a deputy badge and tossed it on the desk top. 'Pin that on your shirt and raise your right hand. I'll swear you in as a deputy and you'll have the law on your side. That's the best I can do for you, Taw. I wanta see the end of this business, but right now I'm up a gum tree. Pinning a badge on you and turning you loose on the county just might bring the jigger who framed you out of the woodpile long enough for us to nail him.'

Taw frowned as he gazed at the law star. He fancied the sheriff was joking, but there was no sign of amusement in Whitney's harsh features. The sheriff's face looked as if it had been carved out of the side of a mountain.

'Go on. Pick it up and pin it on,' Whitney advised. 'We'll toss the cat among the pigeons and see what happens.'

'I'm an ex-con. You know I can't be a deputy. The townsfolk would burn up if I showed on the street wearing a law badge.'

'I've got to fight fire with fire,' Whitney insisted. 'Just do like I say, Taw, and I'll take the consequences if it goes wrong.'

'If it goes wrong I'll probably be dead,' Taw retorted.

'You'll be dead before the sun comes up if you don't get some protection from me. What have you got to lose? Your life ain't worth a plugged nickel if you try to stand on your own.'

Taw gazed at Whitney's harshly lined face. He nodded slowly and reached out for the law star, pinned it to his shirt front and raised his right hand. Whitney got to his feet and swore him in.

'That's good.' The sheriff nodded. 'Now we'll show ourselves around town and let them see you're working for the law. We're gonna put a number of noses out of joint, and that might flush out the man who's back of all this trouble.'

Taw had his doubts, and wondered if the sheriff was on the level, but he could see there was nothing for it but to go for broke although his life was on the line.

'How's your gun speed?' Whitney queried. 'Five years ago there was no one could shade you when it came to pulling a gun. I guess prison has slowed you some, huh?'

'I've practised every morning since they turned me loose.' Landry shrugged. 'I guess I'm speeding up again. Have you got any idea at all who is behind my troubles? I didn't rob the stage office, and I reckon the man that did is still around. He must have left some clues to his identity.'

'I've gained suspicions over the years, but getting proof is the thing, and we may do that now by twisting the situation around. Someone might get worried enough to try something, and in doing so might show his hand. If we're sharp enough we'll get him.

Come on, let's get out on the street and put a stick in the spokes of the wheel that's been turning against you. But one thing — don't shoot first.'

'That's like tying my gun hand behind my back,' Taw protested. 'Are you setting me up as a target, Sheriff?'

'It comes down to that, I guess, but not in the way you're thinking.' Whitney smiled. 'Just remember that I'll be at your side if trouble starts, and any trouble will likely point in the direction of the man who set you up.'

Taw opened the office door and stepped out into the shadows, his muscles tensed for shooting. Whitney followed him closely and they walked along the street in the direction of the saloon, which was noisy. A group of four men were standing on the sidewalk in front of the batwing doors. A tall figure appeared beyond the four and came forward through the shaft of light emanating from the saloon.

'Here's Barney Crow,' Whitney said. 'He's my deputy.'

Taw recalled that someone had used the name Barney when he was attacked in the alley beside the doctor's house, and he studied the tall figure intently as it came towards them. A straying ray of lamplight played upon a harsh face as the deputy paused within feet of them. He was big, raw-boned, with an angular face that was dominated by a large, bulbous nose set above a sneering mouth.

'What's going on?' Crow demanded. 'That looks like Landry you got there, Ben. What's he doing out here? He oughta be hanging from a beam.'

'Stow it, Barney,' Whitney rapped. 'Landry is wearing a star, and he's gonna help us get at the polecat who's been thumbing his nose at me for the past five years.'

Crow shrugged and turned away. 'I guess you know your own business best,' he said. 'I'll watch the office while you're out of it.'

Whitney moved on and Taw accompanied him, glancing over his shoulder to watch Crow enter the law office, aware that the fingers of his gun hand were tingling. There was danger in this evolving situation and he could only wonder what was in the sheriff's mind and why the situation was turning like a wheel making a full circle. He was only two weeks out of prison and was now wearing a law star.

They reached the saloon and the four men standing in the entrance parted to permit them entrance. Whitney led the way into the building and stalked across to the bar. The interior of the big room was brightly lit, and Taw looked around quickly, noting several faces he knew from the past. No one greeted him, and most of the men present had wooden expressions that gave away nothing of their inner thoughts.

There were two 'tenders behind the long bar, shirt-sleeved and busy. A flight of stairs led up to the first floor, and Taw spotted a shotgun guard seated on a chair on the gallery above. Some two dozen men filled the centre of the saloon, where small tables were set out, most of which were occupied by card-players. Halfway along the bar a small, stunted man, dressed in an immaculate broadcloth suit, stood in the centre of a tight knot of three big men who looked like bodyguards.

Whitney saw the direction of Taw's gaze and leaned towards him as they reached the bar.

'That little guy is Bradley Cadell. He bought this place last year, and has just about taken over the town since he arrived a little under five years ago. He's bought up ranches and owns most of the business in town. Watch out for him. He's running hot, and nobody, but nobody, has stood in his way and survived. Those men around him are hired gunnies, and he's never without at least two of them at any time. I reckon he's got the three of them on duty tonight because you're back in town. Cadell has gotten away with it so far because outwardly he stays within the law.'

Taw studied Cadell's small figure. Despite his lack of stature, the saloon owner exuded an air of arrogance and aggression that was all too plain to Taw's critical gaze. Cadell was talking the loudest of the group, waving his hands to emphasize his words, and his dark eyes were watching the room at large, looking for the slightest hostile variation in the scene around him.

'Do you reckon he's behind my trouble?' Taw queried.

Whitney shrugged a massive shoulder and grimaced. A 'tender came along the bar and Whitney ordered two beers.

'The boss says these are on the house,' the 'tender said, nodding in Cadell's direction as he slid two foaming schooners of beer along the polished bar top.

'Thanks, but I always buy my own beer in this place,' Whitney replied with a grin, and slapped a dollar down on the bar.

'Sorry, I can't take your money,' the 'tender insisted. 'It's more than my job is worth to go against the boss's orders.'

A small man with an over-large stomach and bandy legs moved away from the bar on the far side of Cadell and his three protectors and came along to pause before Whitney. His sun-tanned face was the colour of mahogany and he exuded an implicit air of wide open spaces and faraway mountains. He gazed unsteadily at Taw, who saw at a glance that he was not armed.

'This is Pete Juby, the regular stagecoach driver, and he never talks sense when he's had a few,' Whitney said in an aside to Taw.

'I was about to come and report to you, Sheriff.' Juby's words seemed to tumble and run together as they emerged from his mouth. 'There was an attempt to hold up the stage this afternoon when I reached Black Rock, and the jigger with the gun is this man standing beside you.'

'Who told you to make that accusation, Pete?' Whitney asked.

'What are you getting at?' Juby grimaced. 'No one told me to say anything. I'm reporting what happened at Black Rock this afternoon, and I recognize this man as the one who tried to rob me.'

'What time did the incident occur?' Whitney demanded.

'About four o'clock, near as dammit.'

Whitney nodded, and the ghost of a smile played momentarily around his taut lips. 'I got a wire from Marshal Eke at Oak Creek early this evening telling me that he spoke to Taw Landry in Oak Creek at four-thirty today and Landry said he was on his way here. Seeing that Black Rock is sixty miles from Oak Creek, I figure you're a mite mistaken in your accusation, Pete. Why don't you go find a hole somewhere, crawl inside it, and sleep it off, huh? I'll talk to you again when you're stone-cold sober.'

'Are you calling me a liar?' Juby demanded.

'You figure it out.' Whitney spoke roughly and his eyes glinted. 'Now get

41

out of here, you fat little bastard, and stop wasting my time.' He raised his voice until it rasped into every corner of the big room. 'That goes for everyone who reckons to get in on this trouble. I'll jug the whole dang town if I have to, so you can figure that baiting my new deputy sheriff is not something I'll stand for. Is there anyone who doesn't understand what I'm saying?'

The silence in the saloon was tense. Men gazed impassively at the sheriff, their expressions, closed and their eyes narrowed, and some of them looked sheepish. Taw glanced around, feeling as if he were standing in a long, dark tunnel with no sign of daylight at the end of it. He curbed his impatience and forced himself to go along with Whitney's game.

The batwings creaked, the sound coming loud in the silence. Taw flicked his hard gaze towards the door and saw a man peering into the saloon, eyes shadowed by the brim of a low-pulled Stetson. The muzzle of a pistol showed in the narrow opening of the swing doors, and immediately exploded into smoke and flame. Taw's glass of beer on the bar top shattered and heavy echoes crashed and rolled deafeningly.

Taw drew his gun instinctively, saw the newcomer's pistol lifting for a second shot, and fired, aiming for the gun. His shot rattled bottles and glasses on the bar with its raucous blast. The batwings were pushed open by the gunman, who staggered forward a couple of unsteady steps on stiff legs, his gun falling from his grasp to thud on the floor. Then he twisted and fell heavily, like a sack of grain dropping out of a loft doorway.

Whitney was the first to break the frozen tableau caused by the shock of the action. He paced towards the threshold, bent over the motionless figure and rolled it on its back before straightening to face the motionless room.

'It's Thad Grimmer,' he said. 'It looks like he was seeking revenge for Sadie's murder. I told the fool earlier to leave that chore to me. Now he's got himself shot in the shoulder. This better be a lesson for the whole town. Nobody can take the law into his own hands and get away with it.' He glanced around. 'Mason, cut along to the doc's house and fetch him quick. If he ain't there then bring his daughter. She's good with bullet wounds.'

One of the townsmen left the saloon in a hurry. He stepped over the body of Thad Grimmer and shouldered through the batwings; his boot heels rapped sharply on the sidewalk outside. Whitney came back to the bar, his face set in harsh lines. He looked at the smashed beer glass on the bar top and signalled to a 'tender.

'Let's have another glass of beer here and be quick about it,' he rasped.

Cadell came along the bar with one of his three guards. His fleshy face was impassive but his eyes were narrowed, glittering like a snake's, beady and hostile. The guard was a tall, thin figure with a lean, pock-marked face and dark eyes that were permanently narrowed and filled with aggression. Looking at him, Taw got the impression of a wild dog on a leash waiting to be turned loose to bite and kill.

'You've made your point, Sheriff,' Cadell observed in a voice that sounded like gravel rolling in a creek bottom.

'Are you telling me you've got the message?' Whitney smiled. 'Someone laced this town with poison against Landry. There were twenty men around the street when the sun went down, all armed and ready to gun him down when he showed, or to lynch him. But that ain't gonna happen now. Landry is working for me, and no one will be plumb foolish enough to buck the law and make a try for my new deputy unless he's real desperate.'

'I thought it was not possible for an ex-convict to hold down a law job,' Cadell observed, looking at Taw with an impersonal gaze.

'Why are you so set against him?'

Whitney countered. 'But I guess there's only one reason why you'd want him out of it. You've been trying to get your hands on Dave Landry's ranch, and now Taw is back you're gonna have to admit defeat because Taw won't stand by and watch his father suffer any more.' The sheriff glanced at the motionless gunnie at Cadell's side. 'Turn off the tough attitude, Stagg. You ain't scaring anyone.' He turned his gaze to Taw. 'This is Ike Stagg. You better keep an eye open for him in future. Don't ever let him get behind you or you'll be sorry. Cadell don't feel safe around here without his bully boys backing him.'

Cadell smiled mirthlessly. His eyes were like chips from a fallen star.

'Landry, I hope you'll have more luck than I've found around here,' Cadell said harshly. 'Someone has been sitting on my tail from the moment I rode into Cottonwood, snapping at my heels like a mad dog. I forget the number of times I've reported problems to the law and not received any help.'

'That's because I never turned up anything in my investigations, Cadell.' Whitney shook his head. 'I wasted a lot of time on your say-so, running around chasing after shadows, until I came to the conclusion that what you were telling me was a pack of lies. There's never been anyone dogging you. I never found one shred of evidence, and it's my belief that you kept complaining to cover your own activities. I found more sign against you than for you, and it is bad luck I can't prove any of it.'

Cadell shook his head and sighed with impatience as he turned away and went back along the bar, followed by Ike Stagg, who had gazed fixedly at Taw during the harsh conversation between Cadell and Whitney, his brown eyes filled with potent hostility.

'You want me to take care of Landry, boss?' Stagg asked Cadell in a hoarse tone as they returned to the spot where the other two guards were standing.

'What do you mean, take care of

him?' Cadell demanded.

'I don't know.' Stagg shrugged his shoulders. 'What do you want to happen? Give the orders and I'll carry them out. You've been talking a lot about Taw Landry coming back from prison. Now he's here, and he don't look like much to me.'

'That's your professional opinion, is it?' Cadell countered with a sneer. 'You're a sap-head, Stagg. I've been waiting for Taw Landry's return because he'll take the blame for anything bad that happens around here in the next few weeks. So do me a favour and don't try to use that jumping bean you've got in your head instead of a brain. I got great things planned for the future, and Taw Landry will play a big part in my plans. I can push on now he's back, and we'll have that deadbeat, Whitney, running around in circles. If Landry is innocent of that robbery then the man who did it will have to make a play for him, and I wanta know who the real guilty man is.'

'OK, boss, if that's the way you want it.'

'I'll tell you what I want, Stagg.' Cadell sharpened his tone. 'Tail Taw Landry as from now and watch every step he takes. I want to know everything he does. I need to know if he starts getting close to the truth. Don't let him see you tailing him, and don't let anyone kill him. You got that?'

Stagg nodded and reached for his beer.

Taw drank his beer while gazing at the inert figure of Thad Grimmer lying on the floor with a trickle of blood issuing from his shoulder wound. The air of tension in the big room seemed to relax, but Taw was beset by doubt and uncertainty. He had come home from prison expecting to find his troubles at an end, only to find the nightmare still existing, and now he was knee-deep in it, caught up by what had started five years before.

He became aware that an alarm was nagging in the back of his mind, and

49

considered it until he decided it had come to life when he set eyes on Barney Crow. He was certain the chief deputy had attacked him on the street earlier, and a brief sight of the man had given him the impression that he had seen Crow someplace before today. He scoured his mind but failed to drag the fact from his memory. But he would not let the matter rest. He would work at his doubts until they disclosed themselves.

The batwings swung open and Mason returned with Brenda Elwood at his heels. The girl paused beside the motionless figure of Thad Grimmer, and for a moment her sharp gaze found Taw's impassive face before shifting to the law star pinned on his chest. He saw disapproval flit through her expression before she dropped to her knees beside the wounded man, and he wondered what he had to do to please just one person in Cottonwood.

3

'I guess I've put a stop to the threat against you, Taw,' Whitney said, grinning. 'Have you got some place to stay tonight? You can spend the night in the jail if you like. It'll be safe in there.'

'Thanks, but hearing about what's going on around here, I think I'd better split the breeze to DL and take a look at my pa. I heard he was beaten up a couple of weeks ago. Did you find out who attacked him?'

'No, but I'm still looking into it. I've got a pretty good hold on the town. We don't get much in the way of violence, except that which is directed against folks who stand up to Cadell and his boys.'

'And you say no one is talking about that.' Taw shook his head. 'Surely there's someone ready to stand up and be counted!'

Whitney showed his big teeth in a mirthless grin. 'There have been one or two in the past but when the local bully boys got to work on them they pulled in their horns. But I'm still working on it, and I'll break the deadlock before I'm through.'

'And now you've got a murder to solve.' Taw thought of Sadie Grimmer and a pang filled his breast. He had thought himself to be in love with her five years ago but she had turned her back on him and his predicament, and the passage of time had smothered his emotions. But now the girl was dead, and he could feel the stirring of strong protest in his mind.

'Sadie was killed to put blame on you,' Whitney said. 'You're gonna have to be careful, Taw. There's no telling what will happen next. You'll have to be on your toes all the time.'

Taw nodded. He had no intention of being caught flat-footed.

Brenda arose from checking over Thad Grimmer and spoke to the townsmen who were standing around watching.

'Would some of you carry him along to the doctor's office, please? I need him on the table there.'

Whitney went forward and quickly organized the removal. Grimmer was placed on a table which was carried out of the saloon by four men. Brenda went along with them. Whitney turned to Taw.

'If you're riding out to DL then you better get moving. I'd like you back in my office around nine in the morning. We'll get to work early trying to pin some of these unlawful acts on the men responsible. I'll walk along to the barn with you and see you safely out of town, but after that you'll be on your own, so watch your step.'

Taw was suddenly eager to be gone from town. The set-up around him was too pat for his mind to penetrate. He had no idea what was going on, but realized that the pattern had been set about the time he went to prison. His thoughts were confused as he walked with Whitney to the livery barn, and the sheriff's conversation made little sense to his ears as he prepared his horse for travel.

'Watch your back,' Whitney said when Taw stepped up into his saddle. 'See you in the morning.'

Taw lifted a hand and reined away, setting the horse into a lope which carried him into the surrounding shadows. He hit the trail and swung west; the night was too dark for him to see land-marks, but he could have found his way to the DL ranch blindfold. A faint breeze blew into his face and he travelled at an easy lope, trying to sort his thoughts into some kind of order, but he felt like a man with a noose around his neck and his feet unsteady on an upturned bucket. He had a presentiment that he was standing on the edge of hell.

His alertness was honed to a fine edge, he discovered as he continued. His eyes became accustomed to the gloom and his range of vision increased.

The sky was high and wide, cloudless, and the glittering stars seemed large and over-bright. It did not take him long to sense that he was being followed. He reined off the trail and dismounted to stand in the brush that grew profusely around him, listening intently. The sound of an approaching horse came to his ears and he clamped a hand to his mount's nostrils.

Moments later a rider swept past on the trail and the thud of hoofs sounded loud for some seconds before receding slowly. Taw caught a glimpse of the figure but could not make out any details of the man. He stood in the shadows while his mind considered the possibilities. The rider was likely a cowboy from one of the neighbouring ranches, but Taw was too astute to accept any situation at face value. He was alone against the rest of the county until he could grasp some aspect of what was going on, and until he had some idea he could not afford to take chances.

He remounted and rode on, staying away from the trail although his progress was much slower across country. But he had no intention of riding into an ambush and his ears were strained for hostile sound, his eyes sharpened for trouble.

It was close to midnight when he spotted the shapeless huddle of his father's DL ranch ahead, nestling on undulating rangeland with the blackness of hills forming an impenetrable backdrop. A thin crescent of the moon was peering down at him from the shoulder of a distant peak and a ghostly white light illuminated the rough ground, making vision deceptive. But Taw knew exactly where he was and continued onward steadily, his excitement growing at the thought of seeing his father again.

He rode into the yard. The ranch house was in darkness and stillness lay heavily upon the ranch. He stepped down from the saddle and looped his reins over the hitch rail in front of the porch. A faint creaking sound attracted him and he stiffened, his right hand dropping to the butt of his gun. He realized that a wooden shutter over the nearest window had been opened, and the next instant a guarded voice called a challenge from the deep shadows surrounding the little house.

'Declare yourself, mister. I got a gun on you. Who in hell are you sneaking around here this time of the night?'

Taw recognized his father's voice and relief gusted through him.

'It's Taw, Pa. Sorry I'm so late. I planned to stay in town till morning, but I found trouble there.'

'Taw! Hold on and I'll let you in. I've been hoping you'd show up.'

Taw smiled wryly as he waited in the heavy silence. He heard a bar being removed on the inside of the door and, at that moment he caught the click of a steel-shod hoof striking against a stone somewhere across the yard. He swung around, gun coming to hand like a well-trained animal.

'Hold it, Pa,' he rapped as the door of the house swung inward. 'We got company. Bolt the door again and stay alert. I'll check who's out here.'

The door closed. Another hoofbeat sounded and Taw picked up further sounds. He moved out into the yard, his gun muzzle steady as he looked around.

Orange gun-flame tattered the night with shocking suddenness and shots hammered, echoing through the shadows. Taw heard slugs crackle past him and thud into the front of the house. He dropped to one knee, anger flaring in his breast. This was a hot welcome home and he did not appreciate it. He threw up his gun and fired instinctively at a gun flash. Three guns were shooting at the house, and a rifle inside the building began cracking insistently as Dave Landry opened fire at their assailants. Echoes hammered across the range, the sounds ugly and frightening in the night.

Taw changed his position, for slugs were striking the ground about him. He emptied his gun in a rapid burst of shooting and then lay silent while reloading. One of the unknown gunmen had dropped out of the attack, and Taw prepared to continue his resistance. For some interminable minutes shots were exchanged, and then the attack petered out. Moments later he heard the sound of receding hoofbeats, and he lowered his pistol, his breath rasping in his throat.

'Are you OK, Taw?' Dave Landry called from the house.

'Sure, Pa. I think they've pulled out. Maybe I hit one of them.'

'I'll join you and we'll take a look around.'

The door creaked open and Taw got to his feet, checking his gun as he gazed at his surroundings. The night seemed deceptively dark because his sight was still dazzled by the shooting. Dave Landry came forward, a shapeless figure in the night.

'What's going on around here, Pa?' Taw demanded.

'I sure wish I knew! I've been getting trouble for some time now, but this is the first time they've come to the ranch.'

'I heard about the beating you took in Cottonwood. Who did it, Pa?'

'If I knew that I would have braced the buzzard. He dropped on to me from behind and I never saw a thing.'

'And you got no idea who's behind this?' Taw could feel impatience welling up behind his breast-bone.

'Son, I wouldn't be skulking in this house every night if I had any idea who's back of it. My stock has been run off and the crew is gone. Come on into the house and let me get a look at you. I ain't happy to see you back here. I half-hoped you'd keep moving to other parts when you got out of jail. You can only get yourself killed if you stick around here.'

'I can believe that.' Taw followed his father into the house and closed the door. He dropped the bar into place as Dave struck a match and lit the lamp.

'This place hasn't changed any in the last five years,' he observed, looking around. His gaze ended on his father's face, and he was shocked by the older man's appearance. 'Jeez, what were you hit with?' he demanded. 'You look like you lost an argument with a runaway train!'

'It ain't so bad now.' Dave shrugged his thin shoulders. He lifted a hand to his face. Bruises were still evident but they had toned down over the two weeks since the attack. 'I'm getting about a bit easier now. No bones were broken, but a few got bent, I shouldn't wonder. Say, what's that you're wearing?'

Taw touched the deputy badge pinned to his shirt front. He had forgotten about it, and explained what had happened in town upon his arrival there.

'I can't believe Whitney would pin a badge on you,' Dave declared.

'He saved me from a lot of trouble by doing so. Someone had roused up the whole town against me, and everyone, but everyone, was out on the street looking for a sight of me. There was talk of a lynching if they caught me.'

'So who worked them up to that pitch?'

'I don't know.' Taw shook his head. 'I was hoping you could tell me.'

Dave Landry grimaced. He looked much older than his forty-eight years, and the recent beating he had suffered had sapped his strength. Taw remembered his father as a powerful man who had not known what it was to back down from anyone, but he could see defeat in Dave's eyes and manner, and the sight served only to stiffen his own resolve.

'I wanta check around outside, Pa,' Taw said. 'I think I nailed one of those troublemakers. I need to get to grips with this business. At the moment I feel like a man who's fallen down a well and can't get back up, and whichever way I turn I find a blank wall in front of my nose.'

'I'll cover you,' Dave said. 'I'd sure like to know who is raising hell around here.'

Taw went outside. He drew his pistol and walked across the yard into the direction from which the shots had been fired at the house. He moved slowly, not certain what to expect. He could see fairly well, and paused when a faint movement attracted his gaze.

'I got you covered,' he called. 'Don't try anything.'

'I'm shot through,' an unsteady voice replied. 'You've done for me.'

Taw covered the figure that was down in the dust and went closer. He saw a gun lying discarded nearby and kicked it aside as he walked in.

'I ain't armed now,' the man said. 'You got me fair and square.'

'Who are you?' Taw demanded. 'What were you doing, riding in here and shooting up the place?'

'I'm Art Powley, and I was doing what I got paid for.'

Taw dropped to one knee beside the

man. Dave Landry came out of the house carrying a lantern which he masked with a Stetson. He came to Taw's side and let the light fall upon the wounded man, whose pale shirt front was soaked in blood. The man's face was bearded and his eyes glinted in the lamplight. He looked stricken, like a buffalo that had been brought down by wolves.

'You've done for me,' he gasped. 'You hit me dead centre.'

'Who paid you to ride in here and cause trouble?' Taw asked as his father dropped to his knees to examine the man. 'Tell me who sent you, and why, and you might live to see the sun come up.'

'I can't rightly tell you that.' Powley's voice was filled with pain. 'Don't touch me. I'm on the way out and I know it. Just let me lie, will you?'

'There were two others with you,' Taw persisted. 'Will you name them?'

'I won't do that.' The man jerked and groaned. Blood gushed from his mouth and his heels rapped the hard ground as he died.

Dave straightened. He picked up the lamp and led the way back to the house.

'There's nothing we can do until sun-up,' he said. 'In the morning I'll look for tracks and see if I can trace Powley and his two pards back to where they came from.'

'That's a good idea.' Taw's eyes glinted. 'I'll ride with you; if we can find out where they came from we might be able to get some answers to the questions bothering me. But perhaps you've got some answers yourself, Pa, without knowing it. Has anyone tried to buy you out while I've been away?'

'Only Brad Cadell. He came out here a couple of years ago and offered to buy the spread. That was after most of my stock was run off. But I turned him down, and since then things have been slowly getting worse and worse in this county. When I complained to Sheriff Whitney he looked around for a bit, but could find no proof of any wrongdoing, so that was the end of it as far as he was concerned. I've holed up here like a soldier in a fort, waiting for you to come back, but now you're here I don't know what we can do, except get ourselves killed before this is ended.'

'It'll be better to go down fighting than to run away from it,' Taw said harshly. 'I want to find out who robbed the stage office five years ago and pinned it on me, and I'm gonna get to the bottom of this if it's the last thing I do, but I have no idea where to start looking for the guilty man.'

'I've got about fifty head of cattle penned up in a draw back of the house,' Dave said. 'I watch them night and day. It's all I got left. I'm going out now to check on them. If rustlers do come for them I wanta be ready to nail them. I won't take any more losses without a fight.'

'I'll go with you,' Taw decided. 'I'm back now, and we're gonna fight this together every inch of the way. We might get lucky if we stay on our toes.'

'Get ourselves killed, most likely,' Dave growled.

They left the house by the back door and Dave led the way along a faint trail through the brush. The night was not full dark. Starshine limned their surroundings. Dave carried his rifle and moved swiftly. Taw followed his father closely, alert to the shadows. They had covered about a mile when Dave suddenly went to ground, and Taw followed suit, hearing, as he did so, the heavy sounds of a herd of cattle on the move.

'The buzzards are stealing my steers,' Dave hissed, cocking his rifle. 'Let's go get them, son.'

'Hold on, Pa.' Taw grasped his father's arm. 'I'm thinking it'll be better to follow the rustlers and see where they take the steers rather than kill them and learn nothing. What we need right now is evidence against the man responsible, so let's play it smart, huh?'

Dave was silent for some moments.

'OK,' he said at length. 'We'll do it like you say. Let's go back to the house, grab some supplies and our horses and then take out after those thieves. They're clear of the draw now, but they'll be easy to track. Them cows won't hurry along.'

Taw was relieved that Dave agreed with his plan. They returned to the house and prepared to travel, then rode out back to the draw. The tracks of fifty steers bunched tightly together were fairly plain even in the night, and they rode steadily, determined to locate the herd and learn of its ultimate destination. Taw felt hopeful that the mystery engulfing them would shortly be solved.

Dawn came. They were heading north. They halted on a reverse slope of a ridge and moved up to the crest to check what was ahead. Dave uttered a low cry of relief when they saw his herd being pushed along by four riders.

'We need to get a good look at those men,' Taw said. 'Can you can recognize any of them, Pa?'

68

'Heck, I can recognize one of those horses from here,' Dave retorted. 'That big black with white on its back legs belongs to Bill Temple, and it sure looks like Temple riding it.'

'Bill Temple.' Taw frowned. 'I heard him mentioned in town. Doc Elwood was gonna be out all night attending Mrs Temple. Would that be Bill's wife?'

'Yeah. I heard she is expecting any time now.' Dave spoke through his teeth. 'So what in hell is Temple doing out here rustling my stock while his wife is having his baby? He runs a shoestring spread over to the east, and he's been hit by money troubles, so I heard. It looks like he's taken this way to get out of it.'

'So we'll try and get him alone,' Taw observed. 'They can't be driving those steers very far now in case they're spotted. My guess is that they'll hole them up in a draw someplace and move them on again tonight.'

'You've got it pegged right, son.' Dave nodded. 'I reckon Temple will cut away home soon as he can if his wife is close to having her child.'

'You must have talked it up,' Taw said. 'Temple is pulling out right now.'

Temple had wheeled his horse from the herd and was cantering away to the east. They watched him until he disappeared behind a ridge, then Taw glanced at his father.

'I reckon you can follow the herd on your own, Pa. I'll get after Temple and learn a few things from him. You just follow this bunch and stay out of sight. I'll come back to the trail and catch up with you later, and if those three rustlers are still with the herd we'll take them by surprise.'

'Suits me,' Dave replied. 'Watch your step, Taw. These men will be fighting for their lives when they're cornered, so don't take any chances.'

Taw grinned. 'Be seeing you,' he said. He wheeled his horse away and rode fast to follow Bill Temple.

It was mid-morning when Temple rode into the small yard of a cattle ranch and dismounted in front of a cabin. Taw reined up behind a nearby ridge and watched the rancher looking around before entering the cabin. There were a few head of cattle in a corral off to the left, and two horses were tethered to a rail near the cabin. The place looked run down. Several rails of the fence surrounding the yard were on the ground and an air of neglect was prevalent.

Taw eased back and began to circle the spread, staying out of sight of the cabin until he reached the rear of the building. He dismounted in thick brush and left his horse hobbled in cover. Mindful of the fact that two horses were tied to the hitch rail, he moved in slowly, alert for trouble, his right hand close to the butt of his holstered pistol. He gained the rear of the cabin and paused, listening intently, and heard the mutter of voices coming from within.

There was a window in the rear wall, and it was ajar. Taw moved to it and risked a peep inside. He ducked back instantly, but not before he had seen a woman lying in a bed and Bill Temple standing beside her. A second man was standing at the foot of the bed, and Taw risked another look to check. He recognized the second man as Doc Elwood, and heard a baby cry as he moved back.

At that moment a gun muzzle jabbed against Taw's spine, and he heard three clicks as the weapon was cocked.

'Who in hell are you, mister?' a harsh voice demanded. 'What are you doing sneaking around here? Get your hands up or I'll plug you.'

4

'Make a move and I'll split your spine.' The muzzle jabbed Taw again, and then a hand grasped the butt of his gun and whisked it clear of its holster. 'That's better. Now you can turn around. You better have a good excuse for skulking around here.'

Taw turned slowly and faced his captor. The man was tall and thin, dressed in range-stained clothes. His angular face bristled with a black beard and his brown eyes were filled with suspicion. His gaze dropped to the law star glinting on Taw's chest and his expression changed instantly, surprise flooding his eyes.

'Are you a deputy?' he demanded.

'Yeah,' Taw replied. 'Maybe you'll tell me why you're ready to pull a gun on a visitor.'

'I saw you sneaking around out here

73

and figured you were up to no good. Why didn't you ride into the yard openly?'

Taw held out his hand for his gun but the man shook his head.

'Nothing doing,' he rapped. 'Back away from that window.' He waited until Taw had complied and then moved closer himself. 'Hey, Bill,' he called. 'Come on out here, huh?'

Temple came to the window and peered out. He gazed at Taw, took in the deputy badge on his chest, and shock showed momentarily on his face.

'I'll be right out,' he replied, turning away.

Taw watched his captor with exasperation flaring in his mind. He heard Temple's boots out front, saw his captor begin to turn to look round in anticipation of Temple's arrival, and he exploded into action. He lunged forward, his left hand reaching for the man's gun. The man caught his movement and swung his gun, but the edge of Taw's left hand struck the gun wrist and deflected the weapon, which exploded as it was forced away. The bullet thudded into the wall of the shack close to the window. Taw slid his fingers around the man's wrist and wrenched the gun from his grasp. He slammed the barrel against the man's head, and pivoted to cover Temple as he appeared around the front corner of the cabin.

'What the hell is going on?' Temple demanded. He was in his early thirties, tall and thin, with a lean face and unblinking brown eyes.

'I came here to ask you that question,' Taw countered. 'I followed you last night, when you and three others stole a herd of fifty head from the DL.'

'Does Sheriff Whitney know what you're doing?' Temple demanded.

'He'll learn all about it when I tote you and your pards into Cottonwood,' Taw retorted.

'I ain't going anywhere.' Temple shook his head. 'My wife has just had a baby and I got to stay here.'

'You should have thought of that before riding out to steal cows. Where were you taking those steers?'

Temple inched his hand towards the butt of his holstered gun.

'You better put your hands up before you make a bad mistake,' Taw told him. 'I'll shoot you if you resist, and that kid of yours will be an orphan before he's twenty-four hours old.'

Temple lifted his hands shoulder high. The man on the ground was stirring, shaking his head and gingerly feeling his skull where the barrel of the pistol had struck him. Taw walked around Temple and relieved him of his gun. The window in the back wall was pushed open wide and Doc Elwood stuck his head out.

'That bullet came through the wall and just missed the crib with the baby in it,' Elwood said angrily. 'If you're going to celebrate then do it out on the range where you've got more space.' He paused, staring at Taw. 'Say, you're Taw

Landry! So you got home at last, huh? And already you're raising hell again. There's a woman trying to rest in here after a very difficult labour.' He shifted his gaze to Temple, noted the man's discomfiture, and shook his head. 'I thought you would have had more sense than to play games at this time.'

'There'll be no more shooting,' Taw promised. 'I'm gonna take Temple into town.'

'It's a joke, ain't it; you wearing a law badge?' Elwood demanded.

'Temple ain't laughing,' Taw retorted.

'I'm riding back to town myself very shortly.' The doctor shook his head. 'If you take Temple then Mrs Temple will be left here alone. That's not good, Taw. She needs someone to take care of her, even if it is only her ham-fisted husband. What do you want Temple for?'

'Rustling. I caught him red-handed last night.'

'Leave him here until I can get my daughter to come out,' Elwood said.

'He won't run away and leave his family. You can pick him up again later.'

Taw nodded slowly. 'OK. I'll go along with that, Doc. Temple, you better be here when I come back for you.'

'I won't leave,' Temple said.

'Who is Art Powley?' Taw asked, thinking of the man he had killed in the night at the DL.

'Art Powley?' Temple shook his head. 'I ain't never heard of him. Who's he?'

'Never mind for now. I'm leaving, Temple, but I'll be coming back for you.' Taw looked at the man sitting on the ground staring up at him. 'What's your name, mister?' he asked.

'Joe Pettit. I got nothing to do with rustling. I help Temple out around here but I ain't got a hand in anything crooked.'

'I'll remember your face.' Taw glanced at Temple. 'Come with me,' he commanded. 'I'll leave you when I hit my saddle. You better stay here and keep your nose clean until I come back, and next time you better have some answers to the questions bothering me.'

Temple said nothing, and accompanied Taw to where Taw's horse was waiting. Taw swung into his saddle and holstered his pistol.

'Go on, get back to the cabin,' he rapped. 'I'll see you later.'

He wheeled the buckskin and rode off in the direction of the stolen herd. When he had put a ridge behind him he proceeded at a gallop along Temple's trail from the herd. He settled down to a lope that covered the ground quickly, and had travelled about two miles when a shot echoed on his back trail. He wheeled his mount and rode back, pistol in hand. As he topped a rise he saw a man down on the ground and a brown horse standing close by.

Taw looked around carefully. There was no movement anywhere. He glanced at the fallen man and saw a Winchester lying on the ground close to an outstretched hand. He moved closer and stepped down from his saddle. He could see the man was dead with a

bloodstain in the centre of his back.
When he turned the man over he found
himself looking into the face of Joe
Pettit, who had braced him at Temple's
cabin.

What was Pettit doing here with his
rifle out of its scabbard? The question
hit Taw hard, but he didn't need to
think twice about an answer. Pettit had
been about to shoot him in the back.
But who had shot Pettit? Again, Taw felt
the irresistible pull of impatience in the
back of his mind, for he was up against
another blank wall.

Taw looked around long and hard,
checking all the likely spots where the
bullet that had killed Pettit might have
come from. Someone had stopped
Pettit from killing him, but for what
reason? Taw shook his head and
remounted to continue. The mystery
was not getting any clearer, and he
could not waste time looking for
answers that were not readily available.
He needed to get back to his father. He
would never forgive himself if anything

happened to the older man.

When he picked up the trail of the stolen herd, Taw looked around eagerly. He rode steadily, following tracks, and it was early afternoon when he topped a rise and saw the trail heading into a draw on his left. He approached cautiously, hand close to the butt of his pistol. The draw led him through a maze of rocks in a defile before it widened out into a grassy area surrounded by low hills. The entrance was blocked with brush, but beyond it the stolen herd was grazing quietly, tired after its travels.

Taw looked around for his father but Dave Landry was nowhere to be seen. Taw moved back along the draw to look for horse-tracks. He quickly found three sets of tracks moving away to the north — the direction the herd had taken from the DL, but there was no sign of Dave's horse. Taw sat his mount and gazed around for movement, trying to work out what his father would have done when the herd had stopped.

Had Dave followed the rustlers to locate their destination? With that thought in mind, Taw rode back along the trail left by the herd until he reached the nearest high ground. He cast around for the track of a single horse, and eventually found some hoof-prints in the dust of a neighbouring slope. He began to trail them, found where they had stopped when the herd entered the draw, and then continued when they went on, dogging the tracks left by the rustlers.

Taw tried to recall the lay-out of the county in this area. There were a number of small ranches in the direction he was taking and he pushed on fast, wanting to overhaul his father before Dave caught up with the rustlers. He was concerned that Dave would take action when it was unwise to do so.

The smell of wood smoke suddenly reeked in his nostrils and he changed direction slightly to ride directly into the breeze. As he neared the top of a long slope, his father called his name from cover, and Taw was relieved when Dave stood up, rifle in hand, and waved.

'Glad to see you, Taw,' Dave greeted. 'How'd you make out with Temple?'

Taw dismounted. His father had made camp in the cover of a stand of trees, and a coffee pot was bubbling on a small fire beside a pan that contained cooking food.

'I saw you from a long way back,' Dave said. 'Come and eat. It's been a long day.'

Taw could not argue with that, and while he appeased his hunger he told Dave of his actions since they parted. Dave listened intently, and when Taw had finished his account his father explained events from his point of view.

'I trailed the herd to where the rustlers hid them,' Dave said. 'I guess you found them penned up, huh?'

'Sure. Then I picked up your trail and followed you here. What happened to the rustlers?'

'There's a cattle ranch about two miles north of here. They rode in, unsaddled, and settled down. I saw about six men about the place, but I got no idea who they are. The ranch used to belong to old Will Garrett. I heard Will died about three years ago, and I don't know who bought the place. But we do know where the rustlers are, and I reckon the best thing you can do is go back to town and raise a posse to come in and clean out those thieves.'

Taw agreed. 'We'd better get away from here soon as we can. We'll both head for town. I don't like the idea of leaving you at the DL on your own.'

'I'll go back to DL,' Dave said in a tone that indicated he would not change his mind.

Taw did not argue. They broke camp and began the ride back to the home ranch. It was close to sundown when they rode into the DL yard, and Taw dropped his hand to the butt of his pistol when he saw three horses

84

standing at the hitch rail in front of the house.

'We got company, Pa,' Taw observed.

'Yeah,' Dave growled. 'And that big grey looks like the hoss Barney Crow rides. He's Whitney's deputy. Wonder what he's doin' here?'

'Looking for me, I guess.' Taw grimaced. 'I was supposed to be in town at nine this morning. Whitney must be wondering what's happened to me.'

As they reined up in front of the house Crow stepped out to the porch, followed by two tough-looking men. The trio stood motionless; hard faces impassive.

'We've been waiting a couple of hours, hoping you'd show up, Landry.' Crow looked massive in the growing shadows. 'Whitney got a mite worried when you didn't show up in town this morning.'

Dave explained the events of the day. Taw watched Crow, wondering where he had seen the big deputy before. He was certain they had met, but his mind seemed clouded and he could not recall the details.

'You're talking about the Garrett place,' Crow said when Dave fell silent.

'Will Garrett died three years ago,' Dave said.

'Sure, and the spread was bought by Cadell. So the rustlers rode in there and made themselves at home, huh?' Crow nodded. 'We'll ride over there and grab 'em. This is the first break we've had. You've done good, Taw. Whitney will be pleased when you tell him about this. You better get back to Cottonwood and report to him. We'll take care of the rustlers.'

'I oughta ride back to the Temple place and pick up Temple,' Taw said. 'He was with the rustlers, and he must have sent Joe Pettit after me when I left his spread.'

'And you reckon someone shot Pettit before he could shoot you.' Crow compressed his lips, and Taw fancied that the big deputy did not believe his account of what had occurred.

'That's how I read the signs. I didn't have time to cast around for Pettit's killer, but I'll get back there at sun-up and look for tracks.'

'No.' Crow shook his head. 'I'll take care of that. You head back to town soon as you can.'

Taw stood silent while Crow and his two companions tightened their cinches and prepared to ride out. Crow swung into his saddle, lifted a big hand in farewell, and rode out fast into the growing shadows. Taw shook his head, feeling uneasy about the situation.

'Who are those two men with Crow, Pa?' he asked when the trio had faded into the background.

'Pete Todd and Frank Weir — a couple of gunnies who ride with all the posses Whitney sends out. I don't like the look of them, but they don't seem to cause any trouble around town.'

'And where did Crow come from? He wasn't around before I went to prison.'

'I don't know anything about him.' Dave shook his head. 'I went into town one day just after you were taken away, and Crow was there, larger than life, strutting around with a deputy badge on his chest. I must say he's done a good job since he joined Whitney, but I don't cotton to him. There's something about him that grates in my mind.'

'I've got a feeling I've seen him before somewhere, but I can't place him at the moment.' Taw frowned as he scoured his memory again. There seemed to be a blank spot in his mind where Crow was concerned. 'I'd better ride into town, Pa,' he continued. 'I need to check with the sheriff. Why don't you come in with me? I sure don't like the idea of you being out here alone after what's happened.'

'I'll be OK, son.' Dave spoke firmly. 'I've been out here alone for the last five years.'

'But I'm back now, and trouble is sparking. I'd feel a whole lot easier if you stayed close to me.'

Dave shook his head. 'I got to get my herd back tomorrow,' he said. 'Frank Jackson and his outfit will help me. You remember Jackson, don't you?'

'Sure.' Taw nodded. 'I gotta be riding, Pa. Don't take any chances out here. Art Powley's sidekicks could turn up again.'

'I'd welcome the chance to trade some more lead with them buzzards,' Dave retorted.

Taw took his leave and picked up the trail to Cottonwood. Full dark came as he cantered through the night. His thoughts were busy but seemed to be going around in circles in his brain. He was overtired and mentally strained when he reach town and made for the livery barn. There was a light in the law office window, but the main street was gloomy, the only bright spot being Cadell's saloon, which was busy.

He dismounted outside the barn and let the buckskin drink at the trough outside the main door. A lantern was alight just inside the entrance, and Taw eased his pistol in its holster when he led the horse inside, for the surrounding shadows were impenetrable. He took good care of the buckskin. The silence around him was overpowering, not at all like the previous evening when he had arrived.

When he moved to the big main door a man stepped into the open space and Taw dropped a hand to his pistol.

'Is that you, Taw?' the man demanded. He had advanced until the lantern was just behind his right shoulder, which put his face in deep shadow.

'Who are you?' Taw countered.

'Andy Ward. Don't tell me you've forgotten me, Taw. We were the best of pards before they hauled you off to jail.'

'Yeah.' Taw relaxed slightly but his hand stayed near the butt of his gun. 'How you doin', Andy?'

'I've been hanging around waiting for you to get back,' Ward said. 'You could be in a lot of trouble, Taw. You remember Rick Allen?'

'Sure. What's with Rick?'

'He's been in Cadell's saloon all evening, likkerin' up like there'll be no tomorrow. He was always sweet on Sadie Grimmer, even when you were walking out with her, and he picked up with her after you went to jail. They were planning on getting hitched in a couple of months. Now Sadie is dead, and Rick figures you killed her. He's been making bad threats against you.'

Taw compressed his lips. 'Have you got any idea what happened to Sadie?' he asked.

'Whitney has been around town all day, asking that question, and nobody, but nobody, has got any idea. Most folk in town think you had something to do with it even if you didn't actually kill her. They figure your return has sparked off more trouble.'

'Thanks for the warning, Andy. I got an alibi for the time Sadie was killed, and I have no idea who would want her dead.'

'Watch out for Rick,' Ward said. 'He ain't in any state to listen to reason.

91

He'll pull his gun on you if he sees you. Me, I'm heading for home. See you around.'

Taw nodded and left the stable. He walked along the street to the law office. A sigh gusted from him as he opened the door and entered. Sheriff Whitney was seated at his desk, and his chair scraped back as he sprang up.

'Where in hell have you been, Taw?' he demanded. 'I've been thinking all kinds of bad things have happened to you. You shoulda come into town first thing to report, and then you could have gone off on your own.'

Taw explained the incidents which had occurred when he reached the DL the night before. Whitney listened impassively, shaking his head from time to time. When Taw lapsed into silence Whitney cleared his throat.

'Looks like you had more than your share to cope with,' he said. 'So Temple has got himself into trouble, huh? And you reckon he sent Pettit out to gun you down. So who shot Pettit? Did you have a guardian angel riding your back trail today?'

'Don't you believe me?' Taw demanded.

'I ain't calling you a liar.' Whitney sighed. 'You got a right to defend yourself, and if Pettit had his rifle out then he was sure intending to take a shot at someone. But who in hell shot him?'

'I reckoned Pettit was after me. I was the only one around. It's been one helluva day, Sheriff, and right now I'm bushed. I need some food and then a night's sleep.'

'Sure. I've got to make a round of the town so I'll walk to the diner with you, in case Allen is watching for you.'

'I hear you've been asking questions around town about Sadie's death,' Taw said. 'Have you got anything on that?'

'Nary a thing! I checked out the witnesses who heard Sadie screaming in her cabin, and I can't believe nobody went to check on her. Then she fell silent, and that was it until Thad Grimmer visited her shortly after, found her dead, and raised the alarm.'

'Rick Allen was planning to marry Sadie,' Taw observed. 'Was anyone else interested in her?'

'I see what you're getting at, but I don't think that's the direction to go for her killer.' Whitney gnawed his bottom lip as he considered. 'Her death came right out of the blue, and there are no pointers to the killer.'

'And I guess most folk around here suspect me, huh?'

'Bill Tarleton doesn't. He's put you in the clear. He eats supper at Maggie Brown's guest house every night seven days a week and you can set your watch by him. He sits down at Maggie's table dead on eight, so if he saw you on his way out of the stable then you're in the clear as far as killing Sadie is concerned.'

'So why was she killed?' Taw mused.

'I figure that's the only way to approach the slaying.' Whitney grimaced. 'Sadie kept herself to herself. She was planning to marry Rick Allen, and no one else was on the scene. I've got nothing yet, but I ain't giving up. Come on let's see you into the diner. Where are you gonna sleep tonight? I need to know where you are at all times, just in case someone else around town turns up dead.'

'An empty cell will do,' Taw said. 'But if you don't want me for anything I could ride back to DL and help my pa get his herd back. I got a bad feeling about him being alone out at the ranch.'

'Your return to the county has sure sparked off a heap of trouble, and someone is back of it, pulling strings. But we'll smoke him out, Taw. Just go along with it for now and we'll get some proof before long.'

They left the office and walked along the street to the diner. The rush hour was over and there were vacant tables inside. Taw entered while the sheriff went about his duties. A waitress approached him, looking tired and strained after a long day. She took Taw's order and went into the kitchen. Taw tried to relax, but had too much on his mind. A torrent of unanswered questions was flooding through his thoughts and he was unable to halt it. He was still grappling with the mystery when the waitress brought his meal.

The hot food did much to restore his spirits, and he was relaxed enough to take his time over his coffee, but tiredness was pulling at his mind when at last he arose to go back to the law office with the intention of sleeping in an empty cell. He pulled open the street door of the diner and stepped out into the shadows of the street, and for once his alertness was not at full strength. He paused, still in the light issuing from the diner, and took his time to look around at the encroaching shadows; then all hell broke loose.

Gun flashes split the darkness from across the street and heavy Colt-fire boomed. The big diner window was shattered instantly.

Taw felt the flashing pain of a

bullet-strike in his left thigh as he hurled himself down off the sidewalk. His gun was in his hand by the time he lay in deep shadow, listening to a string of slugs thudding into the front of the diner . . .

5

Pain spread through Taw's left leg and he could feel blood trickling across his thigh just above the knee. He lay just off the sidewalk in the dust of the street. Two guns were firing at him from the alley opposite the diner. He refrained from replying to the shooting while he removed his dusty neckerchief and felt for the wound in his leg. He found a torn area in his pants just above the knee, which was soggy with blood. He tied his neckerchief tightly around the wound.

A gun opened fire from across the street to his left but the slugs were aimed at the alley mouth where the ambushers were sited. Taw watched, his gun unfired in his hand. The two ambushers returned fire, and then silence swooped in and echoes faded. Taw remained motionless, watching and listening.

He heard footsteps in the alley across the way. The ambushers were pulling out. He tried to penetrate the shadows to the left but failed to see anything. He waited, aware that time was on his side. Moments later he saw a figure emerge from the shadows to the left and start across the street away from the diner. It had to be the man who had fought off the ambushers.

Taw frowned as he pushed himself to his feet. His left leg was painful and refused to take his full weight. He started along the sidewalk, limping badly and having to walk on the toes only of the injured leg. He followed the figure ahead, and saw the man turn into Cadell's saloon. Taw moved in, and as he reached the batwings they were thrust open from inside and Bill Tarleton, the liveryman, emerged.

Tarleton paused. The light issuing from the saloon shone full in Taw's face.

'Howdy, Taw?' Tarleton greeted. 'You were lucky last night that I saw you ride into town or you would have been saddled with Sadie Grimmer's murder.'

'Thanks, Bill, for speaking out. Most men around here would have kept quiet.'

'I know you're more sinned against than sinning. You had a bad break when the stage office was robbed.'

'Do you have any idea who pulled that job?'

Tarleton shook his head. 'I would have come forward if I had,' he said.

'Someone entered the saloon just before you came out. Who was it?'

'Ike Stagg and he smelt of gun smoke.'

'Thanks. See you around.'

Taw went into the saloon and paused on the threshold. His gaze flickered around the large room. There were about twenty men inside, and no one seemed to be interested in the shooting which had occurred. Cadell was standing at the bar and Ike Stagg was with the saloon man, talking rapidly.

Mindful of the silence that coincided

with his arrival, Taw limped along the bar to Stagg's side. The gunnie looked round as Taw reached him, and dropped a hand to his gun, but Taw's hand shot out and reached the butt of the weapon a split second before Stagg could touch it. He drew the weapon with a slick motion and sniffed at the muzzle.

'It was you on the street just now,' Taw said. 'I was shot at by two men in the alley opposite the diner, and someone cut loose at them from my left. You saw them off, Stagg, and I wanta know why you took my part.'

'I happened to be on the spot and I saw you come out of the diner,' Stagg said easily. 'When those two opened up at you I joined in because you're a lawman. Ain't that what a good citizen is supposed to do?'

'And did you just happen to be on the spot this morning at the Temple spread when Joe Pettit figured to take a shot at me?'

'Hell no! I ain't been out of town at

all today.' Stagg shook his head.

'Someone has been riding my tail ever since I left town yesterday,' Taw observed. He glanced at the impassive saloon man. 'What's going on, Cadell? Stagg wouldn't do anything unless he had your say-so. What are you up to?'

Cadell grimaced. His face was composed as he looked into Taw's eyes. He shook his head.

'I guess I figured you'd had enough grief with what happened five years ago, so I reckoned to ease your return a little by setting Stagg to watch your back. Twice he's done you a big favour.'

'Thanks.' Taw nodded. 'I won't forget that. Did you shoot Pettit this morning, Stagg?'

'He was fixing to shoot you in the back.' Stagg shrugged. 'I stopped him the only way I could. Are you gonna arrest me?'

Taw shook his head. 'You saved my life. But I ain't satisfied about your reason for doing so.'

'I had orders from the boss.'

'So why did you set Stagg on my tail, Cadell?'

'I told you. I reckon you didn't rob the stage office five years ago. You got a bad deal there and I'd like to know who pulled that job. I reckon you're the only one around here who is likely to get at the truth.'

'I think you've got a bad motive for stepping in and I want to know what it is.' Taw insisted, his tone sharp. His wound was hurting badly and his patience was low.

Cadell shook his head. 'You're barking up the wrong tree. I'm on your side, feller, and I can prove it. Come into my office.'

Mystified, Taw followed Cadell to the rear of the saloon. Cadell opened the door of his office and stepped inside. Taw followed closely. The office had a desk in it, a filing cabinet, and a leather couch. Taw halted quickly in shock, for Rick Allen was stretched out on the couch, snoring softly, and there was a bruise on his forehead.

'An old friend of yours, I believe,' Cadell said, smiling thinly. 'He was in the saloon most of today, drinking steadily and uttering threats about what he was gonna do when he met up with you. He got so damned obnoxious this evening he began to annoy my customers. I asked him to leave but he said he was waiting for you to show up. Then he turned real nasty and my boys had to quieten him down. We put him in here to sleep it off, but I didn't figure to turn him loose tomorrow because he's got a fixation about you. He reckons you killed Sadie Grimmer. So you better lock him up and try to talk some sense into him when he's sober.'

Taw shook his head. He had pegged Cadell as being against him, but the saloon man's actions were those of an honest, law-abiding citizen and he could not fault him, unless . . . He cut off the thought. Cadell was the only man in town who had acted as if he believed in Taw's innocence.

'I'll get Rick to the jail,' he mused.

'I'll keep him in tonight and see what kind of an attitude he'll have in the morning.'

★   ★   ★

'What's going on?' Sheriff Whitney appeared in the office doorway behind Taw. He was hatless, had blood on his face, and was covered with bits of straw.

'What happened to you, Sheriff?' Taw demanded.

'I walked into a gun barrel down at the livery barn.' Whitney spoke through his teeth. 'I never knew a thing until I came to my senses a few minutes ago. Has anything bad happened in town? I must have been attacked with good reason. Someone wanted me out of the way, I guess.'

Taw explained about the shooting outside the diner. Whitney put a hand to his head as if unable to take in the development.

'So that's it, huh?' He stifled a groan. His face was pale. 'They were after you,

Taw. And Ike Stagg was on hand to help you? I'll never believe that; not in a hundred years! So what is Ricky Allen doing, sleeping on your couch, Cadell?

Taw listened to Cadell's account of Allen's actions in the saloon and was inclined to believe that the saloon man was telling the truth. But he didn't pretend to understand half of what was going on and his thoughts were confused. He stood with most of his weight on his right leg, trying to ignore the pain stabbing through his left thigh.

Whitney crossed to the unconscious Allen and shook him by the shoulder.

'Come on, you drunken bum! Wake up! You're in bad trouble, boy, raising hell in my town.'

Allen did not move and, when Whitney attempted to pull the man to his feet the sheriff almost overbalanced. He staggered and reeled back from the couch, lifting a hand to his head.

'You need to see the doctor,' Taw observed.

'I guess you're right.' Whitney straightened. 'Can I leave you to handle this, Taw? I'll see the doc and then get to bed and sleep this off. You can sleep in the jail tonight. I'll see you in the morning.'

'OK.' Taw nodded. 'I'll handle it.'

The sheriff handed Taw a key to the law office before he departed unsteadily, a hand to his bruised head.

'I'll get you some help with Allen.' Cadell glanced at Stagg, who was standing motionless in the doorway of the office. 'Ike, get a couple of the boys to carry Allen to the jail, and stick around there if Taw needs any further help. It looks to me like some of the secrets of the past are preparing to come out, and we must do what we can to help the law.' He snapped his fingers when Stagg did not move. 'Come on, get a move on,' he rapped. 'Taw looks like he needs to see the doctor, so stand by in the law office until he can settle down for the night.'

Stagg and two men carried Allen out

of the saloon. Taw followed to the law office. He unlocked the door to let them in and found the keys to the cells on a corner of the sheriff's desk. Allen was locked in a cell. Stagg and his companions departed. Taw locked the street door and sat down at the desk.

His thoughts ran unchecked over the situation as he saw it. He had been surprised, shocked even, to learn that Allen had taken up with Sadie after he was jailed. He'd had no idea Allen was interested in the girl, and wondered for how long Allen had been attracted. He cast his mind back to the night of the robbery. He had come to town to see Sadie, he recalled, but she was out when he visited her home. Her father, Thad Grimmer, said she was visiting with a friend, and Taw was angry because he'd had a long ride for nothing. He wondered who the friend was whom Sadie visited, thinking at the time that it was one of the town girls. But supposing it had been Allen, who had always been one for the girls and knew how to treat them?

Taw got up and went into the cell block. He looked at Allen huddled on the bunk in a cell and wondered about his motives. Allen's father, Henry, owned the big general store, and Rick had never been short of money. Thinking about it now, it came back to Taw that Sadie had, around that time, become restless in her attitude towards him. He remembered that she tried to get him to leave the ranch and take a job in town, and hadn't spoken to him for a week when he refused. It came back to him that he had not been surprised when Sadie dropped him after his arrest.

His thoughts ran on, following the same trend, and he could recall a number of incidents that pointed to Sadie's waning interest in him. Had Allen felt so strongly about Sadie that he wanted Taw Landry out of his way? Taw shook his head, unwilling to believe the worst of a close friend. But Allen had been drinking all day, with the obvious intention of facing Taw and shooting him. Did Allen really believe Taw had killed Sadie upon his return, despite Bill Tarleton's evidence? And if Allen knew of Tarleton's evidence, then why was he so determined to shoot his old friend?

Taw was aware that someone had set him up to take the blame for the stage office robbery. A wad of greenbacks in a bank wrapper had been found hidden in the barn out at the DL ranch and that piece of damning evidence had clinched Taw's guilt. Taw had always wondered why he had been singled out as a scapegoat. The mystery robber had to be someone with a grudge against him, but over the years he had been unable to pin-point anyone who fitted the bill — until Rick Allen had emerged from the woodwork, and his actions spoke of a deep interest in the current proceedings.

Taw unlocked the cell and entered. He shook Allen without response. Allen was out to the world and reeking of whiskey. Taw shook him again and Allen groaned. His eyelids flickered and, when they opened, his eyes were watery and unfocused.

'Come on, Rick. I need to talk to you.' Taw dragged Allen upright, still shaking him but getting little response.

'Lemme sleep.' Allen groaned and tried to flop back on the bunk but Taw held him upright.

'Wake up! I wanta know why you were in the saloon waiting to gun me down. I thought we were friends.'

'Friends?' Allen stiffened momentarily. He suddenly became animated and his eyes flickered open, but he was unable to fix his gaze on Taw's face. 'I hate you, Landry. I was glad when you went to jail. It got you out of the picture. But five years behind bars wasn't long enough. You had to come back before I could marry Sadie.'

Taw was shocked by the degree of hatred in Allen's voice.

'And you believe I came back and killed Sadie, huh?'

'Who else did it? She was all right until you got back.'

'Didn't you hear that Bill Tarleton saw me at the livery barn at about the moment Sadie was being killed in her cabin? I couldn't have been in two places at once.'

'Tarleton must have lied.' Allen dropped back on the bunk as Taw released his grip, and began to snore.

Taw went back to the office. He had plenty to think about. How had that wad of stolen money got into the barn out at the DL ranch? And how had the sheriff known it was there? Taw well remembered the morning when Whitney turned up at the ranch with a posse. The sheriff had gone straight into the barn and found the money. So someone must have told him where he would find it.

Impatience filled Taw and he paced the office as he tried to make sense out of the thoughts seething through his brain. He had been too shocked five years ago to ask some of the questions bothering him now, but he would ask them soon, and insist on getting answers.

Taw stifled a yawn. He had had no sleep the previous night and felt the need to rest. He checked that he was securely locked in the office, then went through to the cell block and stretched out on the bunk in an empty cell. At first he thought he would not be able to sleep under the pressure of his thoughts and the pain in his thigh, but he closed his eyes determinedly and the next thing he knew someone was banging insistently on the street door of the office.

The first rays of the morning sun were peeping in at a window when Taw arose from the bunk. He almost lost his balance when he put his weight on his left leg for the limb had stiffened during the night, and he paused to examine it. At least the bleeding had stopped! He limped through the office to the street door, unlocked it, and Barney Crow came thrusting forward to enter.

'Where's the sheriff?' Crow demanded.

Taw explained the incidents of the

previous night and Crow shrugged his wide shoulders.

'Trust Whitney to find trouble just when I need him,' Crow said savagely. 'I'm the only one around here who does any law dealing.'

'What happened about the rustlers?' Taw asked.

'They were gone when we got to Cadell's ranch. We had that ride for nothing. So we cut off east and went to Temple's place, but he wasn't there either, just the nurse taking care of Mrs Temple. We swung back to where your father's rustled herd was penned up, thinking the rustlers might have taken it on from there, but the steers were still in that meadow. There was nothing else for it but to come back here empty handed. Now I'm gonna get me some breakfast and then hit the hay. When you see Whitney, tell him what I did.'

The deputy departed swiftly, and Taw watched him striding along the sidewalk. He could not believe the rustlers had gone. They had not known they

114

were being traced. And would Temple have made a run for it, leaving his wife and new-born child? Taw did not think so, and he was thoughtful and confused by events. He had no idea what was happening behind the scenes of normal life in the county.

Taw picked up the bunch of keys and went into the cell block. Allen was snoring. Taw entered the cell and shook the man without result. He relocked the cell door and left the office, locking the street door at his back. The town was quiet and still as he went along to the doctor's house. He needed treatment, and was impatient to ride out to the DL ranch, concerned that his father might have found more trouble during his absence.

Doc Elwood was eating breakfast when Taw walked in on him. The doctor got up immediately and led the way into his office, a small room at the front of his house. Taw sat down on a chair and Elwood washed his hands.

'You've been lucky,' Elwood pronounced

upon examining Taw's wound. 'The bone wasn't touched, but you're gonna need to rest up a few days to give it a chance to heal.'

'There's no chance of that,' Taw replied. 'I wanta ride out to the DL soon as I can. Three men shot up the place while I was there the night before last. I killed one of them. Did you know a man called Art Powley?'

'Can't say I did. Was he the man you killed?'

'That's what he said his name was. He was a stranger to me. Crow returned this morning, and he said Temple has disappeared from his place. He's run out, leaving his wife and baby.'

'Damn! I hope Brenda will be OK out there alone. I thought Temple would stick now his wife has got the baby. I guess he ran out because you were nosing around out there.'

'Don't blame me for Temple's mistakes,' Taw said sharply. 'He was rustling cattle, and he can't get away with that just because his wife has had a baby. He should have thought of the trouble he could find before he took that trail. Did you know he sent Pettit after me when I rode out of his place? And Pettit is dead. Someone was watching my back, and killed Pettit before he could put a slug in me.'

'I didn't know.' Elwood shook his head, his leathery face expressing doubt. 'It's strange how trouble has sprung up since you got home from prison.'

'There's nothing strange about it, Doc. I was framed five years ago, and now I'm back the guilty man has got to cover his tracks again. He knows I'm gonna keep after him until I get him.'

'Or until he kills you,' Elwood amended. 'I won't lie to you, Taw. I always thought you were guilty. The evidence against you was overwhelming. But my daughter Brenda always stood up for you. We had some pretty raw arguments over you. She wouldn't hear one word of your being guilty.'

'Cast your mind back five years,' Taw suggested. 'Look at the situation as if you know I was not guilty and see if you can think of someone who might have robbed that stage office.'

Elwood smiled and shook his head. 'I'd need time to do that properly,' he said. 'Leave it with me for a few days. But thinking about the robbery off the top of my head, I must say there was one fact that has struck me as being significant, although I could never see the point.'

'What was that?' Taw urged.

'How did Whitney know the wad of notes was hidden in your barn? I was with the posse when it came to your ranch five years ago. Whitney did say he knew where the money was hidden, but he didn't say who told him, and he didn't have to look around when we got to the DL. He went straight into the barn and picked up the wad of notes. That didn't strike me as odd at the time, but now we're talking about it, I've got to say it was strange, the way he handled that.'

'I thought the same thing, but not at the time,' Taw admitted. 'But

Whitney handled that business very well, although I was on the receiving end. I must say he always treated me fairly, and didn't spare any effort to check out everything I told him.'

'I'm not like most other men,' Elwood said slowly. 'I'm dedicated to helping the sick, and my job takes me out into some strange places and situations. Take the Temple place. I'm out there, delivering Mrs Temple's baby, and you turn up out of the blue to arrest Temple for rustling. A shot was fired and the bullet came through the wall of the cabin. It only just missed the crib the baby was sleeping in. I'm not blaming you for what happened. If you caught Temple rustling then he should be brought to justice. What I'm getting at is that Mrs Temple was so upset because her new-born child was almost shot that she said things she wouldn't normally have spoken. She railed at Temple for risking their whole way of life, and she did it in front of me. That sort of thing happens all the time. You'd be surprised by some of the secrets that come out into the open when I'm around.'

'But you haven't got any idea who could be at the back of my trouble, huh? OK, Doc. I'd better get back to the jail. When the sheriff turns up I'll be heading out of town again. I'm worried about my pa.'

Elwood shrugged and returned to his breakfast. Taw went out to the street, and was thoughtful as he walked in the early-morning sunlight. He saw a figure standing at the door of the law office and quickened his pace. When he approached the man he recognized Henry Allen, Rick's father.

'I just heard you got my boy behind bars.' Henry Allen was slightly built with narrow, sloping shoulders. His face was craggy, his hair white, and he looked a lot older than his fifty-two years.

'Yeah. He was making a nuisance of himself last evening,' Taw responded.

'He drinks more than is good for him. Is he gonna be charged?'

'That's not up to me. The sheriff will

handle it when he shows up.'

'Is it true Rick was threatening to kill you for murdering Sadie Grimmer?'

'That's what I heard. When I saw Rick he was sleeping it off in Cadell's office. I put him behind bars for his own safety. Do you wanta talk to him?'

'Not right now. I got to open the store. Keep him locked in until he's sobered up. I'll talk to Whitney when I've got more time.'

Taw frowned when Allen turned on his heel and hurried away, then went into the office and looked in on his still-sleeping prisoner. Rick Allen was out to the world. Taw shook his head and decided to get himself some breakfast. He left the office and was locking the street door when a gun muzzle jabbed him in the back. He froze but turned his head slightly to see who was behind him. Shock hit him hard when he found himself looking into the ashen face of Thad Grimmer, who was pressing the muzzle of a pistol against his spine.

6

'What's on your mind, Thad?' Taw demanded. 'You look like you should be in bed, resting that shoulder of yours.'

'I can't rest while the man who killed my daughter is walking the street,' Grimmer retorted.

'Do you know who killed Sadie?' Taw challenged.

'You did. You came back from prison and killed her because she was gonna wed Rick Allen.'

'Is that what you think? Well, I got news for you. I didn't know she was seeing Rick until after she was killed and I'll tell you once again that I didn't kill her. I was putting my horse in the livery barn at about the time she was murdered. I saw Bill Tarleton at that time, and he told the sheriff.'

'If you didn't kill Sadie then who did? There's no one else around here with anything against my girl.'

'The man who killed her must have thought he had. I didn't even know Sadie was living in a cabin. When I went to prison she was living with you at the back of your gun shop. So when did she move out of your place?'

'She started going around with Rick Allen but they were always fighting like cat and dog. It was bad to hear them. When I stepped in to put a stop to them, Sadie went completely off the rails. She moved out, and we hardly spoke a word after that. But she was still my daughter, and I wanta get the man who killed her.'

'That makes two of us, Thad, so put away your gun and try to think about this with your head and not your heart. You won't get very far if you can't see past the appearances. I want to get the man who killed her as much as you do, and if we work together we might be able to put a rope around his neck.'

'I figured you for the killer,' Grimmer said obstinately.

'That's why the killer struck at the time he did,' Taw mused. 'He knew I was odds on to take the blame. So put up your gun and we'll see what we can do about getting him. I'm about to go to breakfast. Why don't you join me?'

Grimmer shook his head. 'I don't feel like eating. I'll hold my fire on you while I look around some more, but I ain't got a clear mind where you're concerned.'

'Have you talked to whoever heard Sadie screaming in her cabin? That's the place to start. Someone caught her at home and killed her, and he must have left some sign.'

'I tried to go into the cabin but Whitney stopped me — said there might be clues to the killer and I could wipe them out. But I need to do something. I'll go out of my mind if I have to stand back and do nothing.'

'I've got Rick Allen in the jail,' Taw said. 'Why don't you come in and talk to him? He should be awake now. He might talk to you where he would clam up if I asked him anything.'

'Do you think he might have killed her?'

'The only thing I know is that I didn't kill her, and that fact puts me one step ahead of everyone. From where I'm standing it looks like every man in town is a suspect. That's where we have to start from, and the sooner we get things moving the better.'

'If Rick killed her I'll shoot his eyes out! He was always arguing with her, I don't know what she saw in him.'

Taw unlocked the door of the office again and entered. Grimmer followed, and Taw paused by the desk.

'You're gonna have to leave your gun out here,' Taw said.

Grimmer looked down at his gun and then laid it down on the desk. He looked at Taw with sudden hope in his eyes, and Taw could gauge the degree of shock and pain the man was suffering.

'Let's try and find out where Rick was at the time Sadie was killed,' Taw said.

He took the cell keys and led the way into the cell block. Allen was lying on his back, snoring, out to the world. Taw tried to rouse the man but Allen was still out, and Taw shook his head.

'It looks like he ain't gonna be in a position to talk for hours,' he mused. 'Why don't you come back later?'

Grimmer nodded reluctantly and turned away. Taw locked the connecting door between office and cells. Grimmer did not pause. He walked to the street door and departed. Taw watched him go with growing sympathy in his heart.

He left the office and went along to the diner, feeling ravenous. After a good meal his spirits were restored and he began to make plans. He needed to talk to the sheriff, for in the back of his mind was a nagging fear about his father's safety. He was aware that a devious plot was unfolding around him; could feel its sinuous coils surrounding him, but there were no obvious clues to the man or men controlling it.

He stood for a moment outside the

diner, wondering what to do next, and had started back to the law office when a stagecoach appeared at the end of the street, raising dust as it jolted its way to the stage depot. As he walked towards it Taw spotted the diminutive figure of Pete Juby, the driver, sitting on the high seat, and a pang stabbed through him when he recalled Juby's accusation in the saloon.

Juby stepped down from the coach and hurried into the stage office. Taw reached the coach as Juby reappeared. Juby halted in mid-stride. He gaped at Taw with sudden apprehension, then sprang up into his seat on the coach.

'Hold it,' Taw rapped. 'I wanta talk to you, Juby.'

'I ain't got time right now,' Juby retorted, snatching up his reins.

Taw palmed his gun and tilted the muzzle. Juby started back in his seat like a frightened yearling, his face expressing horror.

'Get down,' Taw ordered. 'You started something the other night and I mean to get some answers from you.'

'I made a mistake,' Juby said quickly. 'There was a robber who looked just like you. I guess I thought it was you because of your reputation.'

'Come on down and we'll talk about it,' Taw insisted.

'I'm running late this morning. Can't it wait until I get back tomorrow?'

'If you don't get down I'll put a bullet in your arm and jug you for resisting arrest.' Taw waggled his pistol.

Juby came off the driving seat as if it had suddenly turned hot. He stood in front of Taw, his expression reflecting utter fright.

'That's better,' Taw remarked. 'You've known me for years, Juby, so I don't think you made a mistake when you accused me of holding up your coach. Who put you up to lying about me?'

'I don't know what you're talking about.' Juby shook his head. 'So it wasn't you! OK! I admit I made a mistake.'

'You made a mistake by accusing me

in the first place. Now you better start telling the truth or you'll see the inside of the jail.'

'I got to get the stage moving.' Juby looked around desperately. 'You can't hold me up. I got mails aboard. You'll be in trouble if you delay them.'

'What's going on here?' a voice demanded, and Taw looked round to see Ben Simmons, the depot manager, standing in the doorway of the stage office. 'Juby, why ain't you raising dust?' Simmons rasped. 'You're ten minutes late already. If you ain't fit to drive because you got loaded last night then I'll put another driver up on that seat — someone who can get the stage rolling on time. I'm tired of your excuses. You've had your last chance.'

'You better replace him,' Taw suggested, 'because he ain't going anywhere until he's answered my questions.'

Simmons glared at Taw, his narrowed eyes resting for a moment on the deputy badge pinned to Taw's shirt.

'So it's you,' he observed. 'I heard

about the accusation Juby made against you. He made a mistake. When he drinks too much he makes mistakes. Now let him hit the trail and roll this coach outa town.'

'OK.' Taw grinned. 'If this is the way you want it, Juby. Turn around and head for the jail. I'm taking you in. I got some questions to ask you and we'll do it with you behind bars.'

'Where is Sheriff Whitney?' Simmons demanded. 'What the hell do you know about the law? You were in prison two weeks ago. Hell, you robbed this office five years ago, and now you're parading around town like you're lily-white. You got a nerve, coming back here like nothing ever happened. Whitney has got a lot to answer for, pinning a badge on you and turning you loose on the town.'

'What are you trying to cover up?' Taw demanded. 'I ain't forgetting that you ran this stage office five years ago, Simmons.'

'What are you accusing me of?' Simmons blustered, his face turning ugly with rage. 'Are you hinting that I know something about the robbery?'

'I was jailed, and I didn't know a thing about it,' Taw grimaced. 'It's about time the town got to the bottom of what really happened. Go on, Juby, you know where the jail is so head for it, and you better get it straight that I'm gonna have the truth out of you.'

Taw was aware that several townsmen had been attracted to the coach by the raised voices, and he saw Cadell standing in the background with Ike Stagg, watching the incident. He pushed Juby hard and the little coach driver almost lost his balance.

'Get moving,' he rapped. 'I wanta know who put you up to accusing me of trying to rob the coach at Black Rock.'

'I told you I made a mistake about that,' Juby protested.

Simmons put out a hand and grasped Taw's left arm.

'You better stop and think about what you're doing?' Simmons said harshly. 'You're getting yourself into a bad spot, Landry.'

'You're about to make life hard for yourself,' Taw replied, shaking off the restraining hand. 'You can come along to the office if you're of a mind to obstruct me.'

'I need Juby to take this coach out. You can talk to him when he gets back from this trip. The drunken fool doesn't know anything.'

'I'll find out exactly what he does know.' Taw pushed Juby again and the man staggered along the sidewalk in the direction of the law office.

'I'll have a word with Whitney,' Simmons called after him. 'You won't be wearing that badge much longer.'

Taw saw Cadell and Stagg turn away and enter the saloon. He pushed the protesting Juby along the sidewalk until they reached the door of the law office, then unlocked the door and thrust his prisoner inside. He followed closely and dropped the bar on the inside of the door. Juby staggered to a chair set before the desk and dropped into it. He produced a large handkerchief and mopped his sweating face.

'So who put you up to accusing me of attempted robbery?' Taw demanded, walking around the desk and dropping into the seat behind it. He laid his pistol on the desk and kept his hand close to the butt. Juby squirmed in his seat, his eyes showing a hunted expression.

'I got to take that stage out,' he said.

'Sure, and you can do that when you've answered my questions,' Taw rasped. 'If you won't tell me then I'll lock you in a cell and throw away the key, so bear that in mind before you clam up.'

'I thought it was you.' Juby screwed up his face into a grimace of despair. 'I guess I do drink too much. I can't remember things from one day to another.'

'So someone put you up to making a false accusation against me but you can't remember who,' Taw suggested.

'I don't know anything, I tell you. Why don't you let me be?'

'Because I need to know what's been going on around town since the stage office robbery and so far you're the only man who's made a slip. Everything else fits neatly around me as the guilty man, and I won't rest until I get at the truth.'

'Well, I can't help you.' Juby set his jaw doggedly and his eyes narrowed. 'You can't hold me in here. I ain't done a damn thing.'

Taw took a tight rein on his impatience. He studied Juby for a few moments while the man gazed fixedly at the floor, and found it difficult to control his rising anger. He picked up the bunch of cell keys and started to his feet.

'I'll lock you in a cell and you can think about this for a spell,' he said.

Juby shrank back in his seat, shaking his head. Taw picked up his pistol and thrust it into his holster. He leaned forward to grasp Juby's shoulder, and at that moment the sound of glass shattering nearby startled him. He threw a glance at the side window overlooking the alley beside the jail. He saw a hazy figure at the window, and the muzzle of a pistol was thrusting through the broken pane to cover the office.

Taw shouted a warning but Juby did not move. The pistol started blasting, hammering raucously, filling the office with gun thunder, and gun smoke billowed. Taw hurled himself sideways down to the floor with the desk between him and the window, and reached for his pistol as he dropped beyond the desk. A bullet struck the desk and ploughed through the flimsy woodwork. Taw felt a flashing pain across his left forearm. His ears rang with the detonations, and he counted five shots before the shooting ceased.

He pushed himself to his knees, his ears singing, and lifted his pistol to cover the window. He saw Juby sprawled on his back on the floor, but his attention was fixed on the side window. He cocked his gun but the figure in the alley had already departed. Taw sprang to his feet and ran across the office to the street door. He jerked open the door and tripped over the doorstep in his haste. When he reached the mouth of the alley he paused, narrowing his eyes. The gunman had departed.

Taw glanced around the street, looking for a fleeing figure, but there were only a few men around, and they were all motionless, gazing towards the law office, shocked by the heavy sounds of shooting. Taw ran into the alley and sprinted along its length to the back lots. His heart was pounding when at last he paused and looked around, to see no movement anywhere. The back lots were deserted. A bitter sigh escaped him as his tension seeped away.

He walked back along the alley, recalling the moment when the office window had been broken. The lower panes were covered with glass paper, but he had seen a hazy figure outside. When he reached the street end of the alley he almost bumped into Simmons, the stage office manager, who was carrying a pistol. He paused and grasped the man by the shoulder.

'Did you see anyone run out of this alley just after the shooting?' he demanded.

'Do you mean to tell me that you didn't do it?' Simmons countered. 'No. I didn't see anyone. I was busy trying to find a replacement to take out the stage. Where's Juby? What have you done with him?'

'He's in the office.' Taw ran to the door and peered inside.

Juby was motionless on the floor. A trickle of blood was leaking from his inert body. Taw hurried to the man's side, and heard Simmons utter a curse when he paused to take in the situation. Taw bent over Juby, and saw at a glance that the stage coach driver was dead. He had been struck by several bullets.

'You shot him!' Simmons accused. 'You killed a man in cold blood.'

Taw turned on Simmons, his anger

flaring. He was still holding his pistol, and he jammed the muzzle of the weapon into the man's chest. Simmons backed off but Taw hustled him, and thrust his muzzle under Simmons's nose.

'Smell it,' he commanded. 'Tell me if it's been fired.'

Simmons shook his head. His face was ashen, as if he expected to be shot.

'Well,' Taw demanded. 'Do you smell gun smoke?'

'No.' Simmons shook his head. 'It ain't been fired.'

'Remember that,' Taw rasped. He turned swiftly as a boot sounded on the threshold of the office and saw Crow's big figure standing in the doorway, his law star glinting on his shirt front. The chief deputy's face was dark with suppressed anger and he glared around like a bear awakened from hibernation.

'What the hell is going on here?' Crow demanded. 'This town is getting to be a hellhole.'

Taw explained and Crow walked

across the office to look down at Juby.

'Yeah, he was shot from that window,' Crow declared. 'Have you looked around outside?'

'It was the first thing I did,' Taw replied. 'Right on the heels of the shooting, and I didn't see anyone. I even checked the back lots, but there was no one in sight.'

'What was Juby doing in here?' Crow's eyes were cold and calculating. 'Why didn't he take the stage out?'

'Landry arrested him!' Simmons snarled. 'I reckon that law badge he's wearing went to his head. He was even talking about arresting me!'

'So what's the story?' Crow turned his attention to Taw, who shrugged as he explained the incidents leading up to Juby's arrest.

'Juby was lying about me trying to hold up the coach at Black Rock,' he said, 'so I decided to get the truth outa him.'

'Did anyone other than Simmons see you bring Juby in here?' Crow persisted.

'Sure. There were several men on the street around the stage office, and I saw Cadell and Stagg watching from the front of the saloon. They backed off inside when I brought Juby along here.'

'Give me your gun.' Crow held out his hand and Taw handed him the weapon, butt first.

Crow sniffed the muzzle and then checked the cylinder. He stuck the muzzle none too gently under Simmons's nose.

'This gun ain't been fired recently,' he declared. 'What do you think, Simmons?'

'I already told Landry his gun ain't been fired this morning,' Simmons growled.

'OK. So don't let me hear any rumours about Landry shooting a prisoner in the jail.' Crow returned the pistol to Taw. 'You better get outa town for the rest of today,' he suggested. 'Go find out what your pa is doing about his stolen cattle. Your old man could be in a lot of trouble out on the range while you're grasping at straws around here.'

'The sheriff told me to stick around here until he shows,' Taw said.

'You can forget about that.' Crow shook his head. 'Whitney ain't in a fit state to come on duty this morning. I dropped in on him on my way here, and he's got a bad headache. I told the doc to call on him. I'm giving the orders around here today, so saddle up and head out. I got a lot to do this morning and I don't need you under my feet or getting shot at by persons unknown.'

'Sure.' Taw felt as if a great weight had lifted from his mind. 'I'll ride out now.'

He turned on his heel and left the office before Crow could change his mind. A small crowd had gathered outside the office door, and excited voices called questions to him as he shouldered his way through the curious townsfolk. He made no reply and hurried along to the livery barn. His thoughts were fast-moving as he saddled the buckskin, skimming over recent incidents, and he was far from satisfied with the situation.

Crow was intent upon getting him out of town, and on the face of it the deputy seemed concerned about the dangers inherent in the situation, but Taw fancied there were other reasons why he was being sent out of the centre of events. There were men in town who did not want him to succeed in solving the mystery of the robbery that led to his imprisonment, and two murders had been committed since his return. To his way of thinking he could do more good in town than he could riding the range, despite his concern for his father.

He left the buckskin standing ready saddled in the stall and went out to the street. The crowd in front of the law office was dispersing now, and the big figure of Barney Crow was standing in the doorway, waving a hand as he talked to the townsfolk. Taw considered the deputy, not liking the attitude hardening inside him, and wondered again why he should think he had seen Crow somewhere in the past.

Crow stepped out of the doorway on to the sidewalk, dragging a figure out of the office as he did so. Taw stiffened and a frown crossed his brow. It looked as though Rick Allen was being discharged from the town jail. He saw Crow thrust Allen savagely away from the office. Allen stumbled and sprawled headlong in the dust of the street. Crow stood over the fallen man, talking incessantly, and then turned abruptly, re-entered the office, and slammed the door.

Allen staggered to his feet and made for the alley at the side of the office. He paused and leaned a shoulder against the corner, his head bowed, body unsteady. Taw watched intently, and when Allen reeled into the alley he ran to the rear of the stable and peered across the back lots. Moments later Rick Allen stumbled into view from the alley. He paused to look around, and then a remarkable change came over him. He straightened his shoulders, raised his head, and strode determinedly across the back lots, all signs of his drunken stupor gone from his demeanour.

Taw was shocked by the abrupt change in Allen's behaviour and followed closely, intent on learning more.

7

Allen seemed to be heading for an isolated barn to the rear of the general store where his father, Henry Allen, stored his stock of supplies. He moved steadily, not looking left, right, or behind him as he continued. Taw remained close to the rear of the buildings fronting the street ready to duck into cover should Allen look round, but the man walked fast, impatience showing in his unsteady steps. He reached the barn, opened the big door, and disappeared inside. Taw closed in, moving warily until he reached the right front corner of the ramshackle building.

Taw peered through a crack in a board and adjusted his gaze to the dim interior, which was more than half-filled with supplies and provisions intended for sale in the store. He saw

Allen standing in a rear corner where a number of small kegs were stacked, and watched with mounting interest as Allen knocked a hoop off one and removed its wooden lid. Allen inserted a hand inside the keg and rummaged around for some moments before withdrawing a dusty saddle-bag and banging it to shake off clinging flour.

Allen's movements became feverish as he unbuckled the saddle-bag. Taw blinked when he saw what Allen withdrew from the bag — a wad of greenback bills! Allen shot the contents of the bag on top of a crate. Taw caught his breath. It looked as if Allen had a cache of thousands of dollars.

It came to Taw that the money was from the stage office robbery of five years ago. He moved around the corner to the door, which was half-open, and drew his pistol as he entered. Allen heard his feet on the hard floor and swung around quickly, his hands filled with wads of money.

'Where did you come from?' Allen

demanded. His face was strained, pasty-white, and his eyes looked wild.

'It looks like you got the proceeds there from the stage office robbery,' Taw accused. 'This is the first time I've seen it, and yet I spent five years in jail for it.'

'This has got nothing to do with the stage office.' Allen threw the money on to the crate. 'My pa doesn't trust banks so he keeps his dough in here. It's quite safe in a keg.'

Taw moved closer, his pistol covering Allen's chest. Allen lifted his hands shoulder high. He grinned inanely.

'So what are you doing with your pa's dough?' Taw demanded.

'I'm gonna borrow some. I'm thinking of heading out of this burg. There's nothing around here for me now Sadie is dead.'

'The sheriff will want you to stick around while he investigates Sadie's murder.'

'You reckon I did that? And I got you pegged for it. Sadie was your girl and turned you down flat, so when you came out of prison the first thing you did was kill her.'

'Sadie and me were washed up before I went to jail,' Taw replied sharply. 'You were trying to cut me out even then, Rick. And I've heard about all the arguments you and Sadie got into. I came into town the night of the robbery because Sadie wanted to see me, but when I showed up she was not at home, and I never found out what she did that night or who she saw, but I guess she arranged for me to come in from the ranch so I could be framed with the robbery. You've got a lot to answer for, Rick, and I have the feeling this is a good time for you to start talking.'

'Sadie was a gal who wanted lots of money, and she knew I was a free spender.' Allen grimaced. 'She complained to me that you had no ambition, and was penniless. She was sick of tagging around with you.'

'Is that why you robbed the stage office?' Taw demanded.

'I didn't do it.' Allen shook his head. 'I always thought you did.'

'So how come you got the money, huh? It is from the stage office. Tell me about it, and while you're at it you can explain how that wad of notes got into my father's barn five years ago. I always reckoned we were good pards, Rick, but you stood by and watched them drag me off to prison. That's how much our friendship meant to you. I guess I can see the way of it now. You wanted Sadie and I stood in your way so you framed me with the robbery. Come on, Rick, admit it. Isn't that what happened?'

'You're loco.' Allen shook his head. 'You did the robbery and you served the time in prison, so why can't you admit it? Why are you so keen to paint yourself white? You're an ex-jailbird now, and nothing is gonna change that.'

'I'll prove my innocence if I can lay hands on the guilty man,' Taw rasped. 'And right now you're standing on the hot spot, Rick. I've caught you with the stolen dough, and you're gonna have a tough time wriggling out of the corner I got you in.'

'Take half the dough,' Allen said tensely. 'You've done time for the robbery so you might as well have some of the money. Take five thousand dollars. You could get away from here and live a high old life.'

'What I'm gonna do is take you in and let Whitney and Crow sweat the truth out of you,' Taw said harshly. 'Put that dough back in the saddle-bag and head out to the law office. I've waited a long time for this moment, and now you're gonna spill the beans about the truth of the robbery.'

Allen stared at Taw for a moment, then turned to put the wads of notes back into the saddle-bag. He buckled the flap of the bag and hefted it. His face was showing desperation.

'There's a lot of dough in here, Taw,' he said. 'You've already paid the price for it so you'd be a fool not to take your share.'

'I'm taking it and you to the law

office,' Taw repeated, 'so let's get moving.'

Allen held out the saddle-bag but Taw shook his head.

'I don't want to touch it. You've been caught with it in your possession, Rick. Let's go give it to the law, huh?'

Allen shrugged and came forward to leave the barn. Taw stepped aside, his gun steady in his hand, the black muzzle pointing at Allen's chest. When Allen drew level he swung the saddle-bag in passing, swiping at Taw's gun. The bag struck Taw's forearm. Allen dropped the saddle-bag and lunged sideways at Taw like a wildcat, swinging his fists. His first blow caught Taw on the side of the jaw and lights exploded in Taw's brain. The next instant Allen was grabbing at Taw, encircling him with his long arms before butting Taw in the face with his forehead.

Taw lost his grasp on his pistol as he started to fight back. He dropped to the floor and arched his back as Allen landed on top of him, and then used his strength to hurl Allen aside. He rolled over and gained his knees as Allen lay shaking his head. Taw could feel blood running down his face from a cut on his forehead, and his nose felt as if it were swelling rapidly. He started to his feet, and saw Allen's hands scrabbling on the ground, clawing for the dropped gun.

Allen pushed himself into a sitting position, grasped the pistol by its muzzle and turned the weapon in his hand. As Taw lunged to his feet he heard the clicks of the weapon being cocked. Allen grinned and pointed the gun at Taw.

'This ain't your day, Taw. It looks like you've lost out again.'

Taw tensed himself to leap forward and grapple with Allen, but he was aware that he had little or no chance of success. Allen's trigger finger was clamped around the trigger and his knuckle showed white as he applied pressure to the deadly metal. Taw gave himself up for lost as he stared into the black muzzle of the gun, aware of a dim protest at the injustice of the situation forming in his mind.

A pistol shot blasted through the silence, rattling a loose board in the barn. Taw winced, expecting the smash of hot lead, but Allen jerked and twisted away. He dropped the pistol and fell back, a splotch of blood appearing as if by magic on his shirt in the region of his right shoulder. Taw jerked his head around and saw Ike Stagg standing in the doorway of the barn, a smoking pistol in his right hand, the muzzle angled to point at the ground. Stagg was grinning.

'It looked like you were fixing to take a trip to Boot Hill,' Stagg said easily. 'It's the third time I've stopped someone aiming to kill you. Cadell sure got it right when he reckoned I should watch your back for a spell.'

Taw shook his head in wonder. He crossed to Allen, expecting to find him dead, but Stagg's bullet had struck high in the shoulder and Allen was unconscious, although his eyelids were flickering spasmodically.

'You're fixing to leave town, ain't you?' Stagg asked. 'I watched you saddle up some time ago. Where are you heading when you ride out? If you tell me it will save me the trouble of trailing you.'

'I was planning on riding out to the DL,' Taw said. 'But this business might cause a change of plan.'

'All yesterday Allen was set on shooting you,' Stagg observed. 'I heard him in the saloon uttering threats against you. So he finally got around to trying it. Lucky I was watching, huh?'

'How long have you been watching me?' Taw asked. 'Where were you when Juby was shot down in the law office?'

'I was in the saloon with Cadell when we heard the shooting.' Stagg grimaced. 'I was set for an easy time in town today, but Cadell wanted me to cover you again, and I got into position just before you came out of the office to saddle up your horse.'

Taw shook his head. He picked up

the saddle-bag and hefted it.

'I saw all the dough,' Stagg said. 'It looks like you were telling the truth after all, huh? You didn't rob the stage office.'

'I might be able to prove that now.' Taw moved to the doorway and peered around the back lots. He saw several men approaching the barn, drawn by the sound of the shot. Barney Crow was leading them. 'I don't know what Cadell has in mind, setting you to watch my back, but I do know I'd be dead right now if you hadn't been covering me,' he observed.

'Cadell has been accused of many things since he set up business around here, and he reckoned sparks would fly soon as you got out of prison.' Stagg shrugged. 'He wasn't far wrong, huh? Now he's proving his own innocence by standing up for the law. Cracks are appearing in the frame-up that surrounded you, and pretty soon now the truth will come out.'

Crow strode into the doorway of the

barn, a pistol in his hand. He stared down at the unconscious Allen and then his gimlet-like eyes swivelled to Taw.

'I thought you'd left town,' he said harshly. 'What in hell is going on here?'

Taw tossed the bulging saddle-bag to the deputy and Crow caught it deftly with his left hand. He listened intently to Taw's explanation of events. When Stagg's part in the shooting was revealed, Crow threw a quick glance at the gunman.

'I thought Cadell would be mixed up in this somewhere,' Crow rasped. 'Were you acting on his orders?'

'Sure. If I hadn't been around, Landry would be dead right now.'

Crow turned on the group of townsmen standing around the door.

'One of you go fetch the doc,' he ordered. 'Stagg, you can come along to my office and make a statement. Taw, you better get out of town like I told you to. I'll handle this business. You got work to do around your pa. He could be in bad trouble while you're fooling around here.'

'Fooling around?' Taw repeated. 'It looks to me like I've solved the mystery of the robbery I was sent to prison for.'

'We'll see what comes out of it,' Crow promised.

'I wanta speak to the sheriff before I leave town,' Taw said.

'That ain't possible.' Crow shrugged his wide shoulders. 'That blow to the head he got yesterday might have cracked his skull, so Doc says. Whitney is in bed in his house, and he's got to be kept quiet and still for the next few days. So it's me and you running the law around here until Whitney is on his feet again. I can handle the town, and you'll have to ride out and see what's happening on the range. You can also swing out to Temple's place and pick him up for helping to rustle your pa's steers. So get moving. I hope you have better luck out there than I did.'

Taw looked at the unconscious Rick Allen and eyed the saddle-bag in

Crow's big left hand. He sensed that he should be on hand to witness any new development in the mystery of the stage office robbery, but he could not openly defy Crow. He turned away reluctantly, pushed through the crowd of townsmen outside the barn, and returned to the livery stables, his thoughts teeming with conjecture, for he was certain Sadie's murder was connected to the stolen money.

He mounted his buckskin and rode out of town, picked up the trail to the DL, and sent his mount along at a fast clip. He checked his back trail often but saw no sign of Ike Stagg, although he did not doubt the gunman was somewhere around. He considered what he had learned so far, and fancied he could see how and why the robbery was committed. Rick Allen had planned it to remove Taw from Sadie's life, and it had succeeded only too well.

But Taw was not wholly satisfied with his reasoning, and wished he could have remained in town to follow up the leads that had become apparent. He rode steadily, diverting his mind to the chore now facing him, and was impatient to see his father. He would never have left his father alone if he'd had a choice, and now, as he drew nearer to the DL ranch, his concern for Dave Landry increased with each mile covered.

The ranch lay still and silent under the hot noon sun when Taw reined up at the gate to the yard. He looked around, his keen gaze narrowed and incisive. He opened the gate without dismounting and rode across the yard to the house.

'Hey, Pa!' Taw dismounted and wrapped his reins around a rail.

His voice echoed in the silence, seemed to mock him, and he turned to look at the dust of the yard. He saw a multitude of horse-tracks and walked across to the corral to look for the freshest among them. He found one set of prints which he recognized as belonging to the horse his father had ridden when they pursued the rustlers.

They seemed to be no more than a day old, and he followed them to the gate, noting that they headed off in a westerly direction. He guessed his father had ridden to Frank Jackson's spread for help to fetch in the stolen steers.

Upon his returning to the house for his buckskin, Taw's keen gaze picked out some ominous blood-stains on the porch in front of the door. He was shocked by the sight and moved closer. The stains had dried, and he estimated they had been made the day before. He went into the house, fearing he might find his father dead or wounded, but the place was empty. He departed, filled with worry, swung into his saddle and set out to trail the prints that had headed away from the ranch the day before. He rode alertly, with his hand close to the butt of his holstered gun.

It was the middle of the afternoon when Taw reached Jackson's ranch. The tracks he was following led straight into the yard, and Taw crossed to the house as Frank Jackson emerged from inside the building and paused on the porch. Jackson was tall and powerfully built, with massive shoulders and a granite face. He was carrying a rifle, and its muzzle covered Taw, who reined up in front of the porch.

'You're Taw Landry, ain't you?' Jackson's tone was unfriendly.

'That's right.' Taw sat motionless in his saddle.

'So what do you want? Your pa was here yesterday. He said he needed help to chase some rustlers. I sent him on his way. It don't pay to get mixed up with the crookedness going on in these parts. I've been left alone so far, and I ain't gonna ask for trouble by taking sides.'

'You saw my pa yesterday? Was he all right?' Taw was concerned about the bloodstains he had seen on the porch at the DL.

'There was nothing wrong with him far as I could tell.' Jackson shook his head. 'Now get outa here. I heard you've been in more trouble since you came back to the county.'

'What did you hear and who told you?' Taw asked.

'Is that a law badge you're wearing? That must be some kind of a joke, huh? How long you been outa jail now? Two weeks?'

Taw realized he would get no help from Jackson and swung his horse. His gaze was on the dust of the yard and he saw the tracks he had followed from the DL heading out to the east. He departed swiftly, cantering and following the prints, wondering what had been in his father's mind because of Jackson's bad reception.

The tracks veered to the north when they were clear of Jackson's spread, and it did not take Taw long to decide that his father had headed for the draw where the stolen stock was being held. Shadows were crawling along the ground when he eventually reached the spot and dismounted to look around. He found the prints left by his father's horse, and saw that the steers were still in the meadow where the rustlers had left them. The tracks he had followed from Jackson's spread now headed out to the east, and Taw suppressed his impatience as he followed them.

It was near dark when Taw reached Temple's place. He reined in and stared ahead into the growing shadows. The tracks went on without deviation. Taw looked at the shadows surrounding the cabin and wondered if Bill Temple was there. Crow said Temple had been absent when he checked the place two days before.

Riding closer, Taw kept his gun hand close to the butt of his holstered weapon. He dismounted in front of the cabin. The sun had gone now and the breeze blowing into his face had lost much of its power. He rapped on the door and moved to one side, ready for trouble. There was no reply. Taw tried the door and it opened to his touch. He drew his gun as he crossed the threshold, but could see nothing in the gloom filling the interior of the cabin.

A strange sound from the darkness alerted him and he lifted his gun.

'Who's there?' he called tensely.

A muffled female voice made an unintelligible sound, and some of Taw's tension eased.

'Is that you, Mrs Temple?' he demanded.

The voice replied, sounding as if it were muffled by a gag. Taw felt for a match in his breast pocket, struck it, and looked around for a lamp. There was one on a nearby table and he lit the wick before looking around the interior. The sight of Brenda Elwood gagged and tied to a chair shocked him and he hurried to her side to release her.

'Where is Temple?' Taw demanded. 'Is he still around?'

'No.' Brenda drew a deep breath and made a effort to regain her composure. 'He tied me up before he took Mrs Temple and her baby off in a buckboard. He left me like this to give himself time to get clear. I heard him say he was getting right out of the county.' Brenda chafed her wrists, and opened and closed her mouth several times to ease the pain throbbing through it.

'My pa was here yesterday,' Taw said. 'I've followed his tracks all the way from the DL. Did you see him at all?'

'Sure. Temple hid under the bed with a gun on me when your pa showed up. Dave asked some questions and then rode out, intending to check on the rustlers he had seen at the old Will Garrett place. It was after he had left that Temple tied me and took out with his family. I can't believe he left me here to die. I couldn't get loose, and if you hadn't showed up I could have sat here helpless for months.'

'I should have taken Temple in when I had the chance,' Taw mused, 'but so much was going on when I was last here I just didn't get around to it.'

'Your father said Temple was guilty of rustling his steers.' Brenda shook her head. 'Can you believe a man with a new-born daughter would break the law like that?'

'I can believe anything after my experiences,' Taw said. 'Have you any idea where Temple went?'

Brenda shook her head. 'He headed north, probably to Garrett's old place, which belongs to Cadell now. I'm sure Cadell bought it up when Will Garrett died.'

'Did you see Barney Crow when he came here?' Taw persisted.

'He came looking for Temple, who lit out when he saw Crow coming, and returned after Crow left.'

'Mrs Temple ain't well enough to travel far, is she?' Taw persisted.

'She should be in bed for several more days, and I dare not think of the consequences she might suffer for getting up early. I tried to talk Temple out of moving her but he's got into a bad scrape and doesn't know what to do for the best.'

'You'll go back to town now, huh?' Taw suggested. 'I'll head out to the Garrett place. I'm getting a mite worried about my pa. I saw some bloodstains on the porch at DL. Did he look all right to you when you saw him yesterday?'

'Sure. I didn't see any wounds on him, and he moved easily. I'm sure that blood you saw was not his.'

'I'll see you on your way back to town before I ride out.' Taw turned to the door, jerked it open, and moved into the doorway, anxious to be on his way. He crossed the threshold to step out into the gathering darkness and, as he did so, a gun flash tattered the shadows and the raucous sound of a gun dispelled the heavy silence.

Taw heard the thud of the bullet smacking into the door of the cabin and hurled himself forward out of the doorway. He hit the ground hard outside and rolled to one side as a burst of fire blasted around him.

8

Slugs crackled around Taw as he flattened out. He felt a bullet tug at his holster, and reached for the butt of his gun as he peered around for the positions of the attackers. Three guns were shooting into the cabin and he marked the shadows where muzzle flame was streaking the night. He lifted his pistol to return fire, coldly and without fluster. Gun flashes dazzled his eyes and he blinked and rolled away from the doorway of the cabin as lead streaked and thudded around his tense figure.

Taw emptied his pistol into the shadows, then ducked to reload when his hammer fell upon a used cartridge in the cylinder. He managed to get three fresh bullets into his gun when a voice yelled from the surrounding darkness and the sound of running feet came to his ears. The attackers were moving in to finish him off. He restrained his breathing as he strained his eyes for movement, and when a gun flash briefly illuminated a running figure he aimed and fired instinctively. A fierce sense of triumph darted through him when he heard a man fall heavily.

The remaining two men halted instantly and went down into cover. Taw reloaded his pistol and prepared to continue the fight. He listened to the dying gun echoes and waited for the next move, but for the moment, the attackers seemed to have lost their determination.

'Hey, Frank?' a hoarse voice called suddenly. 'Are you OK?'

Silence followed the query, and Taw grinned tightly as he waited. The silence dragged on, and minutes later the sound of receding hoofs came clearly on the night air. The attackers were pulling out.

Taw pushed himself up on one knee,

his pistol steady in his right hand, and cuffed back his Stetson. His forehead was beaded with sweat. He listened to the receding hoofs until they faded completely and full silence returned, but still he peered around into the dense shadows, wondering if it was a trick to draw him out into the open, but he sensed the attackers had departed. He got to his feet and pushed his back against the wall of the cabin.

'Taw, are you all right?' Brenda called from the doorway of the cabin.

'Sure,' he replied. 'Stay under cover until I've checked out the area. It could be a trick to get me into the open.'

'I heard two horses leaving,' she responded.

'Yeah, I heard them. There were three men out here when the shooting started, and I think I nailed one of them. Stay quiet and I'll look around. This won't take long.'

His eyes became accustomed to the shadows and he started forward with his gun steady in his hand. Silence pressed in heavily around him. The breeze blew into his face. He peered around as he moved out slowly from the cabin, making for the spot where he had downed one of the attackers. His trigger finger was tense, ready to start working the pistol. He paused when he saw a shapeless figure sprawled in the dust just ahead. It was unmoving, but he was not prepared to take any chances.

'I got you covered,' he called. 'Put your hands out where I can see 'em.'

The figure did not respond. Taw moved in closer, gun hand extended, his muzzle covering the figure. Then he saw a discarded pistol lying just out of reach of a hand and darted forward to kick it away. He dropped to one knee beside the man and grabbed at him with his left hand. The man did not move.

Taw's questing fingers found a patch of blood on the man's shirt front. He pressed his hand against the chest, feeling for a heartbeat. There was no movement. The man was dead. Taw sat back on his heels, gazing around into the darkness. He was certain the other two attackers had fled.

'Taw, where are you?' Brenda called anxiously from the doorway of the cabin.

'Over here,' he responded. 'I've got one of them. He's dead. Bring a light, Brenda, so we can see who we've got.'

'Are you sure the other two have gone?' she demanded.

'Yeah. They lit out. I'll cover you.'

He waited with uplifted gun, and moments later Brenda approached him, carrying an oil lamp. Shadows danced as she approached, and Taw was careful not to look into the lamp's yellow glare. Brenda paused at his shoulder and thrust the lamp low over the dead man.

'It's Frank Jackson,' she said in a shocked tone.

'Jackson!' Taw gazed down at the upturned face, recalling his approach to Jackson's cow spread earlier. 'So this is why he turned down my pa's call for help. He must have been in with the rustlers!'

'There has been a lot rustling in the county,' Brenda observed, 'and a number of range men must be involved in it. Bill Temple was one of them, wasn't he?'

'Yeah. We caught him red-handed.' Taw got to his feet. 'I better get over to Cadell's place and see if those rustlers are still there, although Crow said they had gone when he rode in there. If Temple headed there then I'll want to get him.'

'What about his wife and child?' Brenda asked. 'I'll fetch my horse from the barn and ride with you, Taw. I must do what I can for Mrs Temple; she should be in bed right now, not bumping across the range in a buckboard. If Temple isn't careful he'll lose her and the baby.'

Taw walked with her to the barn and she readied her horse for travel.

'I don't think you should ride with

me,' he said firmly. 'You'd better ride back to town.'

'All right. I'll go back to town.' When she was ready to leave Brenda swung lithely into the saddle and dug her heels into the animal's flanks. Taw sighed heavily in relief as she started across the yard, but as she reached the gate a gun boomed from off to the left and a reddish streak of muzzle flame speared through the shadows. The echoes growled sullenly into the distance.

Taw heard Brenda call his name and he set off at a run across the yard, drawing his pistol as he did so. He could see Brenda's horse, and the girl was not in the saddle. Horror stabbed through him when he spotted her lying in the dust. There was no more shooting, and when he reached her he dropped to one knee at her side.

'Are you all right?' His voice shook with fear.

'The bullet went over my head,' Brenda replied shakily. 'I hurt myself jumping out of the saddle. The ground is really hard.'

'So someone is still lurking around out there.' Taw firmed his lips 'You stay down while I check. I'll come back to you.'

He got to his feet, tightened his grip on his pistol, and walked into the shadows on the far side of the gate, making for the spot where he had seen the gunflash. The silence was intense and the night seemed ominous with menace. He had covered some ten yards when the gun fired again. He hurled himself down at the sight of the flash and heard the slug whine past his right ear. His reaction was such that he fired two shots in reply without being aware that he had responded.

Echoes faded slowly. Taw blinked rapidly, for the breeze made his eyes water. He strained his ears for suspicious sound but heard nothing. It came to him then that Ike Stagg had not taken a hand in this grim game. Had Cadell's gunman been ordered to withdraw his support? He had saved Taw's life several times in the past few days, but now Taw was on his own, and he felt desolate as he prepared to go on.

He walked many yards into the shadows without raising any more shots and decided that the ambusher had fled. He went back to the yard to find Brenda standing beside her horse.

'I've been thinking,' she said firmly, 'and I've changed my mind. I'm not going back to town. Mrs Temple will need me when I catch up with her so my duty is plain. I'll ride with you, Taw.'

'I'm gonna travel fast and I've got a lot of ground to cover,' he replied. 'I'll make for the Garrett place. I know Pa saw rustlers there and I expect that's where Temple has made for.'

'I'll keep up with you,' Brenda said, 'but if I can't then I'll follow along behind. I know where the Garrett spread is.'

'I'll get my horse.' Taw walked back to the cabin.

He checked his buckskin, swung into

the saddle, and rode to the gate to find Brenda already mounted and awaiting him. They rode out together, Taw setting a fast pace. He needed to find his father, and the only place Dave Landry could be was at the ranch where he had seen the rustlers.

Miles slipped by under the unfaltering hoofs of their horses, and Taw was impressed by Brenda's ability to ride fast over the darkened range. But eventually she began to lose ground, and after two hours she slowed her horse and called to Taw.

'I don't want to kill my horse,' she said. 'You go on and I'll follow at an easier pace.'

Taw did not slacken speed and soon drew away from her. He glanced back once and saw her still coming along, then the buckskin pulled ahead and he was alone in the night. He knew the limitations of his mount and continued at the killing pace for thirty minutes more before slackening speed. The time was after midnight, he guessed, when at last he spotted yellow light in the distance and knew he had reached the old Garrett ranch.

He halted a hundred yards out from the spread and hobbled his mount before drawing his Winchester from the saddle scabbard. The square of lamplight in a window of the ranch house attracted him and he walked in closer, moving slowly now. His thoughts were busy. This place belonged to Cadell, so who were the rustlers working for? He pondered the question and could discover no logical answer. Suspicion fell naturally on Cadell, but proof was needed before an accusation could be made.

The ranch was silent and still. Taw paused in the shadows surrounding the gateway and looked around carefully, his eyes narrowed against the breeze and his ears strained for any sound. The square of yellow light seemed to mock him, inviting him in for a closer look, and he knew he had to go forward into whatever awaited him.

He circled the yard and slipped between two rails to approach the house from the right-hand side. When he was standing in the darkness against a wall he paused again and listened intently. The ranch was as silent as a graveyard. He eased forward to the front corner of the house and paused again, aware that the time for action was upon him.

Taw stepped on to the porch, and froze when a sun-warped board creaked under his weight. He waited, peering around, but the sound did not alert anyone and he took another step. He gained the front wall beside the lighted window and craned forward for a quick glance through the dusty panes.

He saw Bill Temple in the big room; Mrs Temple was lying on a couch against the far wall, a crib near by contained the new-born baby. Taw shook his head, wondering what kind of a fool Temple was to risk his family as he was doing. He thought of Brenda, who had been nursing Mrs Temple but had been left hogtied back in the cabin. Taw needed no further proof of Bill Temple's callousness.

He stayed flat against the wall beside the window while he considered his next move. Temple looked as if he was set to remain where he was at least until sun-up. So where were the rustlers? He steeled himself to search the spread, but before he could move he heard the sound of a horse approaching the ranch quite casually.

The rider paused at the gate, and Taw heard a man's voice call out a challenge. He stiffened. There was a guard out there in the shadows across the yard.

'I'm Brenda Elwood. I need to see Mrs Temple urgently. Is she here?'

Taw frowned as he listened to the girl's voice. She had been left in dire straits by Bill Temple, but here she was, still trying to do what she could for his wife.

'The Temples are in the house,' the guard replied. 'You better get over there and talk to Bill. From what he said when he arrived he didn't need your help any more.'

'He doesn't, but I'm certain Mrs Temple does,' Brenda replied firmly.

Taw heard the gate creak open and then a rider came through the shadows to the house. He eased to his left away from the window and gained the corner of the building, to step down off the porch and conceal himself in dense shadows. Brenda dismounted in front of the porch, crossed to the door, and knocked loudly.

Temple answered the door, and growled in annoyance when he saw Brenda.

'How'd you get free?' he demanded. 'I thought I'd got you outa my hair. What the hell are you doing here?'

'I'm concerned about Mrs Temple,' Brenda replied, and Taw could not but admire her determination. 'Moving her was not a good idea, Bill. If she gets a fever then nothing will save her. You'd better let me in to look at her. She might need my help right now.'

'Come in then. And keep your voice low or you'll wake the kid. It's been howling most of the day.'

Brenda entered the house and Taw heard the door close. He turned and walked along the wall to the rear corner of the building, and continued until he could gaze into the shadows surrounding the barn and bunkhouse across the yard. He caught a faint movement out there, and saw the guard making a round of the yard. The man disappeared into the shadows around the bunkhouse, and Taw saw a faint light spring into being inside the low building. It flickered for some moments before being extinguished, and then the guard reappeared and angled across the yard almost to the spot where Taw was standing.

Taw shrank back into the shadows as the guard approached. The man paused at the rear corner of the house, and a moment later a match scraped and the faint glow of a cigarette showed. Taw was holding his rifle in his hands, the muzzle pointing in the general direction of the guard. He could see the man's outline plainly enough, and he eased towards him a step, pushing his rifle muzzle forward until it touched the guard's spine.

'Just stand still and I'll pull your fangs,' Taw declared. 'I got you dead to rights.'

The guard froze and slowly raised his hands. Taw reached out, snaked the man's pistol from his holster and tossed it away into the night.

'Have you got any other weapons on you?' Taw demanded. 'If you have then now is the time to get rid of them.'

'I got nothing else.' The man's tone was soft, shocked, and he stood very still.

'I'm looking for Dave Landry. Has he been around here?'

'I ain't seen a soul all day, except the Temples, and I sure wish they had stayed away.'

'Where's the rest of your crew?'

'Out on the range. I don't expect them back for a couple of days.'

'Whose stock are they rustling now?' Taw demanded. He cut in sharply when the guard began to protest loudly. 'I saw your bunch rustling Dave Landry's stock the other day. I trailed Bill Temple from the stolen stock to his place. So don't lie to me. I know what's going on. Dave Landry was seen heading in this direction, so where is he?'

'OK. So he showed up here, but he pulled out when someone fired a coupla shots at him.'

'Was he hit?'

'No. He was out of range, and didn't stop to argue. I reckon he headed for town.'

'Let's go take a look in the bunkhouse and the barn,' Taw suggested, prodding the man with his rifle muzzle. 'Get moving. Don't give me any trouble or I'll put a slug through you. I'm a deputy sheriff, and the law is making a clean sweep on this range.'

The man set off across the yard with

Taw in close attendance. When they reached the bunkhouse, Taw paused.

'Strike a match and light a lamp inside,' he ordered, and the guard obeyed.

Yellow lamplight illuminated the interior of the bunkhouse. Taw looked around swiftly. The place seemed empty, but he saw the huddle of a figure lying under a blanket on a bunk close by.

'Get up,' he called. 'I've got a gun on you.'

The figure did not move and Taw pushed the guard forward.

'Uncover him,' he ordered, 'and get him on his feet.'

The guard moved to the bunk and twitched the blanket aside. Taw was surprised to see a man bound hand and foot, and his surprise turned to shock when he recognized his father. Dave Landry was gagged with a neckerchief. The bruises on his face, received in the beating he'd taken in town, were livid. The guard untied him and removed the gag.

'Are you OK, Pa?' Taw demanded.

'Taw. Sure. I'm fine. I'm glad to see you. The rustlers have gone to move my cattle. If we ride out now we could catch them in the act.'

'Hold your horses, Pa. We can always catch up with those galoots. I want to find out what's going on around here. This is Cadell's ranch, ain't it? Is he back of the rustling?'

'Ask your prisoner.' Dave slid off the bunk. 'I'm gonna get my horse and ride out after the rustlers. I can't afford to lose that stock.' He turned and grasped the guard by the shoulders. 'Where are they gonna move my steers to?' he demanded fiercely. 'You better come clean or you'll be swinging on the end of a rope before the sun shows.'

'I don't know where they are. I was told to stay here and look after the place.'

'Tie him, Pa,' Taw said. 'We can come back to him later. Bill Temple is in the house with his family and Brenda

Elwood. Let's go talk to him.'

'I was out at Temple's place before I came on here,' Dave said, binding the guard with the rope that had held him. 'I ain't had much luck since you left me the other day.'

'You went to the Jackson spread when you left the DL,' Taw prompted. 'I trailed you there.' He explained the incidents that had taken place, and Dave was shocked when he learned that Frank Jackson had been killed attacking the Temple cabin.

'He sure wasn't friendly when I rode in on him asking for help,' Dave said. 'It proves you can't trust anyone these days.'

'One thing puzzles me,' Taw mused. 'When I rode into the DL I found bloodstains on the porch. I reckoned it was your blood, Pa, but you look like you're still in one piece.'

'Yeah.' Dave nodded. 'Someone was prowling around in the night. I heard his boots on the porch and hollered a challenge. He sent a shot through the door which almost tagged me, and I triggered my rifle a coupla times. I heard him ride off, and next morning I saw those bloodstains on the porch, so I know I hit the buzzard. I found his tracks leading out, but I didn't have the time to hunt him down.'

They lifted the bound guard and dumped him on a bunk.

'If you know what's good for your health you won't make a sound in here,' Taw told the man. 'Come on, Pa, let's go visit Temple and hear what he's got to say.'

Dave extinguished the lamp as they left the bunkhouse, and they crossed the yard to the house. Taw grasped his father's arm.

'Leave this to me, Pa,' he advised. 'Brenda Elwood is inside with Mrs Temple, and I don't want any harm to come to them. I'll get the drop on Temple and we'll wring some truth out of him.'

'You go ahead,' Dave replied. 'You're doing fine, son.'

Taw led the way around to the rear of the house. He reached the kitchen door and tried it. The door was unlocked. He opened it silently and stepped into the darkened kitchen, followed closely by his father. A crack of lamplight showed under the door leading to the rest of the house. Taw handed his rifle to Dave and drew his pistol. He pushed open the inner door and found himself standing on the threshold of a big living-room.

Bill Temple was sitting at a long table, a pistol by his right elbow. Brenda was attending Mrs Temple, who was lying on the couch. Taw paused for a moment to steel his nerve.

'OK, Temple,' he rasped, going forward with levelled pistol. 'Just sit still and get your hands up. I don't want any shooting in here.'

Temple was completely surprised. After making an instinctive move towards his gun he froze and raised his hands, his face taking on a closed expression as he eyed Taw's menacing figure.

'You've got a lot of talking to do,' Taw said crisply. 'Get up and come into the kitchen. We can't talk in here.'

Temple got to his feet readily enough. Dave Landry left the room first, and struck a match as he entered the kitchen. He lit a lamp and covered Temple with the rifle he was holding. Taw paused and looked at Brenda, who stood motionless beside the couch. Mrs Temple was awake, her eyes wide and filled with terror as she gazed at the big pistol in Taw's hand.

'Bill ain't a bad man at heart,' Mrs Temple said in a quavering tone. 'He tried to go straight, working all hours God made to make a dollar, but it all got too much for him. Don't blame him for what he's done. He was forced into rustling to stay alive.'

'If he comes clean about what's been going on around here then he might wriggle out of this little the worse for what he's done,' Taw said.

He went into the kitchen. Temple was sitting on a bench under a window, his hands between his knees and his chin on his chest.

'You've got yourself into a tough spot,' Taw observed. 'What will happen to your wife and child if you finish up in prison?'

Temple made no reply.

'We saw you with some of the crew from this spread, rustling my stock,' Dave said angrily. 'You took the last steer I had. I ought to take you outside and hang you from the nearest tree.'

'Hold it, Pa,' Taw cut in. 'Let me do the talking. There are a few things I want to get straight. Temple, you sent Joe Pettit after me the other day when I left your place, and he was killed while fixing to shoot me.'

'I didn't send him! I tried to stop him but he wouldn't listen to me. He said he had to kill you, and there was nothing I could do to stop him.'

'You didn't try to stop him,' Taw said.

'It's nothing to me what others do.' Temple shook his head. 'There's a bad set-up around here, and I ain't the man to buck it.'

'Tell me about it,' Taw suggested.

'You're a deputy so why don't you know?' Temple shook his head. 'If you wanta do a deal then say so. I'll tell you what I know and you let me go free from here with my family. It's the only way I'll talk. I got my wife and child to think of.'

'You've got a deal,' Taw said unhesitatingly. 'But you've got to have something good to deal with. Go ahead and spill what you know and you could be riding out of here at sun-up.'

'It is common knowledge among the rustlers that Barney Crow is running crooked. You must have known him in prison. He was behind bars while you were there. It was because of what he heard you say about this county that he came here when he left jail. He got the job of deputy with Whitney, and never looked back. In five years he's dug himself in so deep you couldn't get him out with a two-handled spade.'

'Barney Crow?' Taw's eyes narrowed. 'Heck, the minute I clapped eyes on him I thought I'd seen him someplace before. You say he was in prison while I was there?'

'He left jail about a week after you went in. I heard him talking to Sam Ketchell a few weeks ago. Ketchell took over running this place for Cadell when the foreman, Pete Turner, was killed in a riding accident. Leastways, that was what they said when they took Turner's body into Cottonwood. Turner was all beat up and they said his horse rolled on him, but I heard whispers that he was killed because he wouldn't go along with the rustling.'

'Is Cadell in on the rustling?' Dave asked. 'This is his spread. Does he know what's going on around here?'

'I don't know. All I know is what I've told you. Crow is running the rustling, but if you ask me about Crow in front of him I'll deny it. He was out at my place later that day you showed up, and warned me to keep my mouth closed, or else. I got my wife and kid to think about now so I'll deny everything I've told you.'

Temple lapsed into silence. Taw stood gazing at the rustler while his mind pecked at the information he had been given. The silence stretched on, and was suddenly broken by the sound of hoof beats rattling the hard ground of the yard. The next instant a hoarse voice was yelling for the guard.

'Heck, that's Sam Ketchell,' Temple said quickly. 'The rustlers are back, and they weren't expected for a couple more days.'

'Come with me.' Taw dragged Temple to his feet and turned swiftly, motioning for his father to remain in the background. He left the kitchen, his left hand on Temple's shoulder, his right hand grasping his pistol, the muzzle of which he pressed tightly against the right side of Temple's neck. 'Out to the porch,' Taw rasped, and hurried Temple to the front door of the house.

Boots pounded the porch, and the

next instant the front door was thrust open. A big man appeared in the door frame, gun in hand. He paused at the sight of Temple, looked at Taw, and lifted his gun fast.

9

Taw lifted his thumb from his gun hammer as Ketchell levelled his pistol into the aim. Taw's gun bucked and blasted, filling the house with thunder. Ketchell jerked under the impact of the bullet that struck him in the chest and his gun fired a shot into the floor as his finger jarred convulsively against his trigger. Gun smoke drifted across the big room. Taw felt Temple begin to twist into resistance and swung his muzzle back to cover him. Temple struck with a lifting right elbow, slamming it against Taw's gun hand, and the big weapon was pushed aside.

Temple seized Taw's wrist and tried to snatch the pistol out of his hand. Taw could hear boots thudding on the porch outside. He took a short step to his right, putting distance between himself and Temple, although Temple was clinging desperately to his gun hand. A man stepped into the doorway from the porch, gun ready, and opened fire without hesitation.

Taw ducked behind Temple, and felt a tremor run through the man as a bullet hit him somewhere in the body. Temple sagged against him, and Taw, trying to get his gun hand free of Temple's deathlike grasp, saw the newcomer in the doorway in the act of triggering his levelled gun again as Temple fell to the floor, leaving Taw exposed.

A rifle cracked sharply from behind Taw. The man in the doorway jerked backwards and pitched head-long out to the porch, his pistol falling from his suddenly slack hand. Dave Landry came up on Taw's left, the muzzle of his rifle smoking, and Taw threw his father a thankful glance.

'Let's go get 'em, Taw,' Dave rasped fiercely. 'There are half a dozen riders in Cadell's crew and they're all crooked, it sounds like. We caught 'em in the act of stealing my cows, so let's give it to them. It's about time someone stood up for law and order around here.'

'It seems like I've been doing just that ever since I came out of prison,' Taw observed, glancing down at the motionless Temple.

There was blood on the Temple's shirt front. He looked to be badly hit, but Taw had no time to find out. He strode forward to the door, intent on beating his father into the open. Gun echoes were fading slowly and there was no more shooting from outside, but Taw sensed trouble was waiting in the darkness.

He lunged through the doorway and hurled himself to the right, going down on the porch as gun flashes split the surrounding shadows. Four guns began shooting rapidly, and Taw could hear slugs slamming into the woodwork of the house. He triggered his gun, eyes narrowed and determination filling him.

Dave Landry paused in the doorway of the house and lifted the rifle to send a stream of 44.40 slugs into the night, aiming at reddish muzzle-flame lancing through the shadows. The thunderous shooting sent echoes tearing across the range.

Taw dropped flat to reload his smoking pistol, and then realized that the opposition had thinned out considerably. Dave was emptying his fifteen-shot magazine with considerable skill, and suddenly there were no more slugs coming to the house. Silence filtered in slowly, the fading gun echoes sounding ominous in the night. A moment later Taw heard two horses departing. He got to his feet, checking his gun as he did so.

'Looks like they got no stomach for an open fight,' Dave observed. 'Do we go after them, Taw?'

'Not right now,' Taw replied. 'Keep a watch on the yard, Pa. I wanta take a look at Temple. He took a slug that was meant for me.'

Dave stood in the shadows of the porch with his back to the house. The muzzle of his rifle moved slowly as he covered the yard. Taw holstered his pistol and went into the house. Brenda was on her knees beside the prostrate Temple, and Mrs Temple was sitting motionless in shock on the couch.

'How is he?' Taw demanded. 'Will he live?'

'Doc might be able to save him.' Brenda sighed heavily. 'He's badly hurt, Taw.'

'I need to get into Cottonwood soon as I can,' Taw mused, thinking of Barney Crow and what he had learned about the deputy. 'We've chased off the rustlers, and I don't think they'll come back in a hurry. I'll leave my pa here to keep an eye on things while I head out fast. I'll send the doc soon as I hit town.'

Dave agreed to remain at the ranch and Taw prepared to take his leave.

'Taw, promise me you won't go after Crow until I can side you,' Dave said worriedly. 'He's got a couple of shadows following him around — Pete Todd and Frank Weir — and they are a couple of tough gunnies. You wouldn't stand a chance against them in an open fight, not the three of them together.'

'I'll bear that in mind, Pa,' Taw said. 'What do you think the two rustlers who fled from here will do now?'

'They won't come back here in a hurry,' Dave replied with a short laugh.

'I'm sure they won't.' Taw nodded. 'They'll head hell for leather for Cottonwood to report to Crow what's happened out here. With any luck I'll catch 'em on the hop.'

He left the ranch with his father's advice ringing in his ears, fetched his horse and hit the trail at a gallop for Cottonwood, following an indistinct trail through the night. His thoughts were fast and furious in his teeming brain. At last he was beginning to see some light at the end of the tunnel. Crow was running the rustling, but what about the sheriff? Was Whitney involved in the crookedness that was rife in the county? It was obvious that Rick Allen had been involved in the stage office robbery, but how had Whitney known where to find the cash that had been planted in the barn at the DL ranch?

Taw was eager to get to grips with those men responsible for his downfall, and hoped that, with Allen in jail and the stage office money recovered, the whole truth would emerge when he applied more pressure to the guilty men.

Two hours of hard riding took Taw within sight of the lights of Cottonwood, and he reined up on the outskirts to consider his immediate actions. Mindful of his father's warning about Crow and his two tough sidekicks, he dismounted at the end of the main street and walked his horse to the stable by way of the back lots. The time was an hour before midnight when he checked his pistol in the stable before leaving and then started along the street.

There was a saddle horse standing at a rail in front of Cadell's saloon. Taw went to it to find the animal had been hard-ridden recently, and surmised that it belonged to one of the two rustlers who had fled from Cadell's ranch. He peered into the saloon over the batwing doors. There were some fifteen men in the building, and Cadell was leaning against the bar with Ike Stagg in close attendance. Taw wondered why Stagg had been withdrawn from the duty of guarding his back.

There was no sign of Crow or the two hardcases who consorted with him. Taw pushed through the batwings and entered the saloon, his right hand close to the butt of his gun. He crossed swiftly to Cadell's side, and saw Stagg nudge Cadell in warning of his arrival.

'I smell gun smoke on you.' Cadell straightened at the bar. His smooth face looked untroubled but there was a gleam of worry in his pale eyes.

'I've just come from your ranch,' Taw said, and waited for a reaction.

'So how are things out there?' Cadell countered. 'I haven't left town in a coon's age, so I rely on reports from my foreman to keep abreast of what's going on.'

'You'll need a new crew to handle your spread.' Taw launched into an explanation of events, and saw shock spread through Cadell's expression. 'There's no doubt about it. Your outfit rustled the last of my pa's cattle and he recognized some of them. Bill Temple was with them, and I followed him to his place the other day while Dave followed the other rustlers right into your yard. When I rode out there today I found your outfit out on the range and my father hogtied in your bunkhouse. Your crew rode in later, shooting without asking questions. Sam Ketchell shot Bill Temple and I nailed Ketchell. We took on the rest of your outfit until the survivors turned and ran.'

Cadell shook his head in disbelief. 'Are you talking about my cow spread?' he demanded when Taw lapsed into silence.

'Sure. Will Garrett's old place. That's the ranch you own, huh?'

Cadell nodded. He glanced at Ike Stagg.

'Take a ride out there in the morning, Ike,' he said, 'and look around.'

'Bill Temple and his family are in your ranch house,' Taw said. 'Temple is hit badly. Brenda Elwood is taking care of him. I've got to send the doc out right away. Are you saying you know nothing about the rustling, Cadell?'

Cadell smiled. 'I'll prove to you before this is finished,' he responded, 'that I know nothing about rustling.'

'I can believe that much,' Taw admitted. 'I know who is running the rustling and I'll take it up with him soon as I can.'

'That's nice to know.' A faint grin touched Cadell's lips. 'I've been taking the blame for a lot of bad things that have happened around here. I guess you know what I'm saying because you got hooked for that robbery five years ago, but now we know Rick Allen was responsible, and he has confessed to killing Sadie Grimmer. Your return triggered a big argument between them, so Allen said, and he killed her when she told him to drop out of her life because she wanted to get back with you.'

'He's confessed?' Taw repeated in a shocked tone.

'That's the word, and there have been rumours about a lynch party for him.'

Taw shook his head. He felt as if a great weight had been lifted from his mind. He gazed into Cadell's watchful face and wondered what was going on in the man's mind.

'I don't blame you for thinking what is on your mind,' Cadell said. 'The bad men around here had to have a scapegoat to carry the weight of their crookedness and they elected me, but there's not one shred of evidence against me, and until you find some then you better give me the benefit of the doubt.'

Taw turned away. He needed to get Doc Elwood moving to visit Bill Temple. He left the saloon and walked quickly to the doctor's house. There was a lamp burning in a window and he rapped at the door. Elwood opened the door and Taw explained the situation out at Cadell's ranch.

'Thank God Brenda is OK,' Elwood said. 'I'll ride out there without delay. Taw, I'm glad recent events here in town have cleared your name of that robbery you were saddled with.'

'I need to talk to Sheriff Whitney,' Taw said. 'How is he, Doc? Has he recovered from that knock on the head?'

'I'm not happy with him, Taw. Whitney is not a well man now. Crow is running the law at the moment, and I have doubts that the sheriff will come back to duty in the near future. He was badly concussed the other night.'

'Have they found the man who hit him?'

'I talked to Crow this afternoon and

207

he says he hasn't learned a thing. I treated Rick Allen in the jail for the wound he received when you arrested him. He's since confessed that he murdered Sadie Grimmer, and Thad Grimmer is breathing fire and brimstone trying to get a lynch party together, but I think it is just talk. He's bad hurt by Sadie's death.'

'I'd better have a word with the sheriff,' Taw mused. 'Be careful how you ride into the ranch when you get there, Doc. My pa is guarding the place, so sing out before you enter the yard.'

The doctor nodded and turned away. Taw went along the darkened street toward the residential area of the town, and as he passed the front of the saloon a big figure emerged from the building and confronted him. He recognized Barney Crow and drew a swift breath as Crow's two sidekicks came through the batwings and flanked the big deputy.

'I just heard from Cadell that you were back in town,' Crow growled. 'So what's been happening out on the range?'

'Someone rode in to tell you about the shooting at Cadell's ranch,' Taw said. 'Two rustlers got away from me, and I reckon that horse standing at the rail there was ridden in by one of them to spread the word that the rustling gang is finished.'

'I ain't heard a thing,' Crow countered, 'only what Cadell just told me. Anyway, I got some news. You caught Rick Allen red-handed with the dough from the stage office robbery, so that clears you of the robbery. Since then Allen has confessed to killing Sadie Grimmer, so that ties up most of the problems around here. I had a word with Sheriff Whitney a few minutes ago and he says to tell you to turn in your badge now you're in the clear. He only gave it to you because he was afraid you'd be killed because of the robbery pinned on you. Now that danger is past and you can forget about the law.'

'I'll keep the badge,' Taw said

instantly. 'I'm involved in putting down the rustling, and I don't want to quit while I'm ahead. The outfit on Cadell's spread is guilty of rustling, although I believe Cadell knows nothing about it. I want to get to the bottom of what's been going on, so leave the badge with me.'

'No can do!' Crow shook his head. 'Gimme that badge, and then you better get out of town. There is some talk of lynching Rick Allen, and you don't wanta get caught up in that. Now you're in the clear you better keep your nose clean.'

Taw gazed into Crow's immobile features. Crow was holding out his hand for the law star, and for a moment Taw was tempted to reveal what he knew about the big deputy. But he did not fancy a show-down with the tough trio facing him until he had spoken to Sheriff Whitney. He stifled a sigh, removed the star from his shirt front, and dropped it into Crow's ready palm.

'You've done a good job around

here,' Crow said. 'I guess the town owes you a vote of thanks. I reckon something will be done for you later, but right now you better try and live a quiet life, just in case.'

'Thanks.' Taw stood motionless while Crow and his two pards turned and walked away along the sidewalk. His mind felt curiously empty and he tried to stir himself mentally. A moment ago he had been filled with the tension of bringing his actions to a satisfactory conclusion, but Crow had deflated him by taking his authority. The law star had been more than a piece of bright metal pinned on his shirt; it had represented the full might of the law backing him.

'Hey, Crow,' a voice called from the shadows just ahead of the three deputies. 'I've been looking for you. I rode in from the ranch. There's been hell to pay. Sam Ketchell is dead, and so are most of the others. I thought you had the law in your pocket, but there was a guy out there, wearing a law star, who shot the hell out of us. I figure he knows now that you're running the rustling, and he'll be around to trade lead with you before morning.'

Taw stiffened. Crow had paused in the light issuing from a saloon window, and Taw saw the big deputy's right elbow bend as he drew his pistol. The weapon exploded, sending echoes buffeting across the town, and a body fell heavily on the sidewalk. Crow had gunned down the rustler! He swung round to confront Taw, who realized with a stab of shock that the deputy was aiming to shoot him.

Taw lunged sideways through the batwings of the saloon as Crow fired, and heard the smack of flying lead striking the doorpost behind him. Moving fast, he ran half the length of the saloon and dived for an alley door on the left. He saw Cadell emerging from a back room, attracted by the shooting, but did not pause. Crow was thrusting through the batwings to enter the saloon, his deadly gun lifting for another shot.

Tensing his muscles for a bullet in the back, Taw hurled himself out through the side door and into the alley. He collided with the opposite wall in his haste, and spun around to face the back lots, his desperate legs carrying him swiftly into the darkness. He dimly heard Crow's voice yelling for his sidekicks to cover the alley.

Taw realized he could not reach the back lots before the hardcases started shooting into the alley, and was giving himself up for lost when he ran into a stack of crates piled beside the wall of the saloon. Without pausing to think, he hurled himself on to the stack, grabbed the edge of the near-flat roof, and swung himself up into the darkness to roll on the roof. He remained still, gun in hand, his breath rasping in his throat. His mind was needle-sharp now, but his thoughts were filled with confusion as he sought to find a clear way through this problem. The darkness around him was comforting, but he knew the slightest noise on his part would bring the hardcases to him.

He needed to confront the sheriff, aware that he could not shoot lawmen, no matter their degree of guilt. He was out of his depth in this situation and needed help. Where could he go to be safe until he could warn the town at large of Crow's complicity with the rustlers?

Boots thudded on the hard ground of the alley and Taw froze, restraining his breathing as the footsteps came closer to his position. Sweat ran down his face, stinging his eyes, and he felt as if the inside of his chest had been flayed with barbed wire.

He risked a peep over the edge of the roof but could see nothing in the dense shadows. His hands trembled and tension filled his mind. One thought went round and round in his brain — he had to get clear of this grim situation.

'Where in hell has he gone?' a harsh voice demanded just below his position on the roof.

'How the hell do I know,' another replied. 'He must have sprouted wings. He sure moved fast when Crow turned on him.'

There was the sound of a man walking into the stack of crates as Taw had done moments earlier, and a spate of curses ensued.

'Do you think he's up on the roof?' someone asked.

'Don't stand there asking stupid questions,' the other replied. 'Climb up there and take a look.'

Taw clenched his right hand around the butt of his pistol and waited. He heard a scrambling sound as one of the two hardcases started climbing up on the crates. Then a head appeared above the edge of the roof only inches from his face and Taw struck viciously with the muzzle of his gun. There was a yell as the long barrel made contact with the head, then a terrific crash as the man lost his balance and fell back into the alley.

An animal instinct to flee from

danger filled Taw. He scrambled to his feet and ran across the roof, intent on putting as much distance as possible between himself and his pursuers. He reached the edge of the roof on the other side of the saloon and launched himself in a desperate leap for the safety of the slightly lower roof of the next building. He cleared the alley easily, but his moving weight was too much for the sun-warped woodwork. A board splintered under his boots and he sprawled heavily. One foot became trapped in the hole that appeared under his boots and he fell helplessly.

10

Taw strained his ears for hostile sound as he freed his foot from the hole in the roof. The woodwork seemed too flimsy to bear his weight and he felt it give a little as he moved. He froze, half-expecting the roof to collapse, but beyond a few ominous creaks it remained stable and he began to ease across its dark expanse to the alley on the further side, pausing from time to time to listen for sounds of pursuit. A breeze was blowing steadily into his face and seemed to baffle his ears, but he heard nothing suspicious and continued until he found the edge of the roof.

Taw holstered his gun and lay flat on the roof, peering down into the darkness of another alley. He strained his ears to pick up any sound while trying to decide on his next move.

Thinking he was safe from pursuit, he was about to slide over the edge of the roof and drop into the alley when he heard thudding boots approaching below. He drew his gun and waited.

'He's long gone by now,' someone complained. 'It's all right for Crow. He'll walk away from this if anything goes wrong, but we ain't got badges to hide behind, and we're the ones who'll get it in the neck. We should pull out, Frank. We ain't got a leg to stand on.'

'Stop your moaning, Pete. Taw Landry is the only one we have to nail. Nobody else around town knows what's been going on, so if we kill him the situation will cool off again.'

'What about Dave Landry? He saw the rustlers and recognized them. That's why Ketchell and most of them are dead. This has gone too far to be hushed up, and if we had the sense we were born with we'd be forking our broncs for some place far from here instead of trying to kill someone who's good enough to put the pair of us on Boot Hill.'

'We couldn't ride far enough if Whitney gets at the truth. The sheriff is a damn fool, oughta turn in his badge and get the hell out. He's the sorriest excuse for a lawman I've ever met. Come on, let's try and finish this off.'

The two men moved on, and Taw remained motionless as they traversed the alley and departed. He waited for full silence to return before swinging his legs over the edge of the roof and lowering his body full length on his arms before relinquishing his hold. He dropped into the alley, landed heavily, and his right leg gave way beneath him. Pain coursed through the limb. He got up and limped quickly to the back lots. The night swallowed him up, and he heard nothing when he paused to check for sounds of pursuit.

It seemed to take an eternity to reach Sheriff Whitney's house, which was located on the west side of the main street beyond the sprawl of business enterprises. Taw stood in the shadows of the house for seemingly long minutes, listening intently. Lamplight shone in a downstairs window, and he hoped Whitney was not in bed. He tried the front door, found it locked, and, not daring to make a noise, skirted the building and approached the kitchen door.

The back door opened to his touch and Taw paused, gun in hand. He listened for several moments to the heavy silence enveloping the house, but a sense of growing urgency pushed him into action. He entered the house, saw a crack of yellow light under a door ahead, and felt his way forward until he encountered woodwork.

Taw opened the door with his left hand and moved quickly into the room, his pistol levelled at the hip. There was movement in the big front room and he saw Sheriff Whitney at a corner table, filling two saddle-bags with possessions. Whitney caught Taw's movement in the doorway and paused in what he was doing. He dropped his right hand to his side, and Taw noted that the lawman was wearing a gunbelt and holstered pistol. He cocked his gun and Whitney froze his action. The sheriff's eyes seemed dull, almost glazed. There was a bandage around his head and he was unsteady on his feet.

'Are you planning a trip, Sheriff?' Taw demanded.

'The doctor advised me to leave town for my health,' Whitney said heavily. 'I was hurt bad the other night when my head was busted. What do you want, Taw? I heard you were out fighting the rustlers.'

'The nest of rustlers on Cadell's ranch is all washed up.' Taw shrugged. 'They're not a problem any more. Bill Temple told me Crow is running the rustling business with a couple of hardcases backing him, and I daren't do anything about him because he took my law badge. He said you told him I should quit what I was doing.'

'Crow! Say, I didn't tell him to throw

you out. What's he playing at?'

'I reckon you know what his game is, Sheriff. You took him on when he showed up around here from prison, just like you took me on when I returned. I'm wondering now why you pinned a badge on me. Was it to have me on hand if you wanted someone to take the blame for some of your wrongdoing?'

'Why would I pin a badge on an ex-convict?' Whitney rasped.

'For the same reason you've been pointing suspicion at Cadell, to cover up your own activities. Cadell is straight. And now Rick Allen is in jail for stealing that dough I went to prison for. How come you couldn't find out that he was guilty?'

'There was no evidence against him,' Whitney muttered.

'And precious little against me, but I got sent to jail.' Taw's voice was taut with suppressed anger. 'Tell me one thing. That morning you showed up at the DL ranch with a posse to arrest me

— what proof did you have that I was guilty?'

'You had told me you came into town on the night of the robbery to see Sadie Grimmer, but when I questioned her she denied having arranged to see you. She said you and she were washed up, and she suspected you of trying to use her as an alibi when you robbed the stage office. She said she heard you discussing the best way to commit the robbery.'

'Not me!' Taw shook his head. 'It's likely she was covering for Rick Allen. But you walked straight into the barn at the DL the day of my arrest and came out with a wad of the stolen money in your hand. I was too shocked at the time to wonder about that, so how did you know the money was there? You didn't even have to search for it. Who told you the dough was in our barn?'

Whitney remained silent. His face had turned pale and he was sweating. He shook his head, then lifted his left hand to press it against his forehead.

'I'm having a little trouble remembering things since I took that crack on the head,' he mumbled, 'and you're talking about five years ago. Forget about it. You're out of prison now and your name has been cleared. It won't do anyone any good, raking over a dead fire. So Crow took your law badge! So what? You can get back to picking up the threads of your life and putting all this behind you. Hell, if you want another law badge you can have mine. I'm quitting and pulling out.'

He lifted his left hand to his shirt front, unpinned his law star, and tossed it on the table. Taw shook his head.

'I can't take that. Did you know Crow was bossing the rustling? It was pretty damn clever, the way he took over Cadell's ranch as a rustlers' roost. Now he's walking around town like he was the sheriff, and you're planning to skip out and get lost. I don't like it, Sheriff. All the signs point to you being involved in this crookedness. I don't think you should leave town right now.

You would do better to stay and face up to what's coming. I've got a nasty feeling you know more about that stage office robbery than ever came out in court.'

Whitney shook his head. 'I'm mighty tired of all this,' he said. 'I'm gonna leave here right now and I ain't coming back. You can do what you damn well like, Taw. Why don't you take my badge and go for Crow and his two sidekicks? Crow has got too big for his boots lately, and he's due for a fall.'

'I've got a better idea,' Taw replied. 'Why don't we go along to the jail and confront Rick Allen? Maybe then the truth will come out. I'd also like to know where Cadell fits into this set-up. Everyone thinks he's guilty of something, but if he's not running the crookedness then who is?'

'Don't look at me!' Whitney shook his head. 'I've run the law around here since before you were born, Taw, and precious little thanks I've had for what I've done. But that don't make no never mind! It's all over now. I'm quitting.'

Taw cocked his gun and Whitney stared at him in disbelief.

'You're gonna take me in?' he demanded.

'That's the way it looks right now.' Taw shook his head. 'I can't let you ride out until I know what's been going on. I swore to uphold the law when you gave me that deputy badge and I owe it to myself and every honest man in town to do the right thing.'

Taw moved forward as he spoke and slid Whitney's gun out of its holster. The sheriff stood motionless, his face betraying shock.

'You must be guilty of breaking the law or you wouldn't be running out,' Taw insisted. 'Let's get along to the jail. I'll stick you in a cell and then take in Crow and his sidekicks. Crow has got some awkward questions to answer. Bill Temple is ready to spill the beans about the whole set-up now.'

'You'll never make it against Crow and his friends,' Whitney said: 'Let me go and you'll be able to concentrate on the real guilty men.'

'No dice!' Taw shook his head. 'Let's get along to the jail.'

He picked up Whitney's saddle-bags and slung them across his left shoulder.

Whitney heaved a sigh and his shoulders slumped. He started towards the front door, but then swung quickly and grabbed Taw's gun hand, pushing the pistol aside as he sledged his right fist against Taw's chin. Taw ducked to his right and avoided much of the power of the punch, but his senses spun from the blow as he wrenched his gun hand out of the sheriff's desperate grasp. The saddle-bags slipped from his left shoulder and fell to the floor.

Taw backed off and hit Whitney with a straight left punch that took the sheriff squarely on the chin. Whitney uttered a cry and fell back instantly, losing his balance and dropping to the floor. Taw shook his head to clear his senses. When he looked down he saw that one of the saddle-bags had fallen upside down, spilling its contents. Among the items of clothing were a dozen wads of greenbacks. Taw picked up one, saw a Wells Fargo wrapper around the money, and looked at Whitney as the sheriff pushed himself to his feet.

'This is some of the money from the stage office robbery,' Taw accused. 'I went to jail for this dough. How did it come into your possession, Sheriff?'

Whitney shook his head. 'If I told you I'd never seen it before you wouldn't believe me, would you?' he countered.

'How come you've got half and Rick Allen had the other half salted away? Did Rick commit the robbery or were you in it with him?'

'That doesn't matter now.' Whitney looked into Taw's eyes. 'It looks like you got me cold. What are you going to do about it?'

'Put you behind bars until I can get to the bottom of it. Let's get along to the jail. Put that stuff back into the saddle-bag and hurry it up.'

Whitney obeyed, and Taw covered the lawman as they left the house.

'Keep to the shadows,' Taw instructed. 'I don't want to walk into Crow and his two pards.'

They traversed the street. There were several men standing in front of the saloon, but the rest of the townsfolk seemed to have retired for the night. Taw kept well to the shadows, and Whitney did not give him any trouble. They reached the law office, where there was a light in the window, and Taw risked a look inside. He saw a tall thin man seated at the desk.

'Who's that inside?' Taw asked Whitney.

'That'll be Brad Mason. He's the night jailer, and comes on duty only if we have a prisoner in the cells. He's here now because Rick Allen is behind bars.'

'OK. Open the door and go inside. Don't get between me and Mason.'

Whitney opened the door of the office and entered, moving to the left.

The night jailer looked up, and smiled when he saw the sheriff.

'Hey, how are you feeling now, Ben?' he called. His gaze shifted to Taw, and his smile faded when he saw the levelled gun in Taw's hand. 'Say, what's going on?' he demanded.

Taw pushed Whitney forward and then dumped the saddle-bags on the desk.

'Take a look in the sheriff's bags, Mason,' he directed.

The night jailer was mystified, but obeyed, and his eyes widened when he found the wads of money.

'What is this?' he demanded.

'You tell me,' Taw countered. 'What does it say on the wrappers?'

'Wells Fargo,' Mason read. 'Is this some of the dough from that stage office robbery?'

'It looks mighty like it.' Taw nodded. 'But if you wanta know exactly what it is then ask the sheriff. I found it in his possession when I stopped him leaving town.'

'You're Taw Landry, ain't you?' Mason frowned as he gazed at Taw. 'You went to prison for stealing this dough five years ago.'

'But I didn't steal it. Rick Allen did, and it looks like the sheriff is mixed up in it somewhere.' Taw motioned with his gun. 'Let's lock the sheriff in a cell. We'll get at the truth come morning.'

'Barney Crow left town twenty minutes ago,' Mason said. 'He said he was heading for Cadell's ranch because there are rustlers out there. I heard him tell Pete Todd and Frank Weir to keep their eyes open for you. Todd went off along the street but Weir is in the cell block right now. He sleeps in there of a night.'

Mason picked up a bunch of keys as he spoke, and moved toward the cells. Taw motioned for Whitney to follow, and covered the sheriff as they entered the adjoining block. Whitney seemed to be resigned to the situation and meekly entered an empty cell. Taw looked around as Mason slammed the door on the sheriff, and saw Rick Allen lying on a bunk in a cell to the right; asleep or unconscious. Allen's chest was heavily bandaged. The crash of the metal door caused the occupant of a cell to the left to sit up and look around angrily.

Taw covered the man. 'You're Frank Weir, huh?' he demanded.

'That's right. What's all the noise about?'

Weir frowned and reached for his pistol, which was lying in its holster on the floor beside the bunk.

'Hold it,' Taw warned. 'You don't need that. Get your hands up.'

Weir froze and raised his hands. Taw entered the cell and picked up the gun.

'Lock the door on him, Mason,' Taw commanded, backing out of the cell. 'He stays in there. He's involved in the rustling, and he was with Todd earlier, trying to kill me.'

'It looks like being a real busy night,' Mason observed, locking Weir in the cell. 'What happens now?'

'How bad is Rick Allen?' Taw moved

to the door of Allen's cell. 'I'd like to talk to him. He could tell me a lot about what's been going on around here in my absence.'

'I heard he admitted killing Sadie Grimmer. Thad Grimmer was here only a few minutes ago, hinting that Rick had fallen in with bad company, but I didn't think his partners in crime could be the local law department.'

'That's the way it looks.' Taw turned away. 'Let's leave it until the morning. Don't take any chances with these men. If Crow has gone out to Cadell's ranch then I'd better head out there, but fast. My pa and Brenda Elwood are there with Bill Temple and his family. My guess is that Crow is going out to silence them.'

'Heck, I wouldn't wanta go up against Crow man to man,' Mason opined.

'I got no choice,' Taw responded. 'There's no one else to take him on.'

He went to the street door, opened it and peered out at the shadows.

'Don't forget about Pete Todd,' Mason warned.

Taw had not forgotten Crow's second sidekick. He stepped out to the sidewalk and closed the office door. Darkness swooped in around him and he turned his face resolutely in the direction of the livery barn, aware that the sooner he caught up with Crow the better. But as he moved away from the office his keen ears caught the sound of a wagon coming along the street at his back. He turned and faded into the shadows.

The wagon came closer, looming up out of the darkness. Taw ducked a little until he could see the driver in silhouette, and a pang stabbed through him when he recognised his father. A woman was at Dave's side, and Taw caught his breath. It was Brenda Elwood. He didn't doubt that the Temple family would be in the back of the wagon, but what were they doing here? And where was Crow? The crooked deputy should have run into the wagon on the trail.

Taw stepped out to the edge of the sidewalk as the wagon rolled to a halt in front of the law office. His gaze flickered around the street.

'Pa,' he called. 'What's going on?'

'Howdy, Taw?' Dave picked up a rifle and stepped down from the driving seat. 'We decided to come on into town. Temple and his family are in the back of the wagon.'

'Have you seen Crow?' Taw demanded. 'He left town some time ago to visit Cadell's ranch. I was about to ride out there after him.'

'I didn't stick to the regular trail.' Dave chuckled harshly. 'I came across country. It was a little rough on Bill Temple, but I reckoned to get here in one piece. So what's been going on?'

'I'll tell you when we get everyone inside the office,' Taw said.

'Hold it right there,' a voice called from the darkness at the rear of the wagon. 'What's going on here?'

Taw dropped a hand to his gun butt.

He saw a figure come forward out of the shadows of the street and pause behind the wagon to peer around it at Taw and his father.

'Who is it, Pa?' Taw hissed.

'He's that no-good Pete Todd.'

'That's all I wanta know.' Taw drew his pistol as Todd came forward.

Todd was carrying a shotgun with the butt in his right armpit and the twin muzzles pointing at the sidewalk.

'Who are you folks?' Todd demanded.

'Drop that gun,' Taw replied. 'I got you covered.'

Todd halted as if he had walked into a wall. Taw was watching the muzzles of the shotgun, and when they began to lift in his direction he triggered a shot. The detonation echoed across the street. Todd jerked under the impact of the heavy slug, lost his hold on the shotgun, and followed it down to the sidewalk. His boots kicked spasmodically on the boards as he died.

'Let's get everyone inside the office,' Taw rapped. He was aware of Brenda standing very close to him. 'I told Doc about Temple being at Cadell's place but I don't know if he rode out yet,' he told her.

Brenda made no reply. She walked to the rear of the wagon and Dave helped her get Bill Temple out. They carried him into the law office. Mason led the way into the cell block and Temple was placed on a bunk in an empty cell.

'Lock him in,' Taw directed.

Dave Landry came into the cells, and a gasp of shock escaped him when he saw Sheriff Whitney sitting on a bunk in a locked cell.

'So they caught up with you at long last, Whitney,' Dave observed.

'Stay here in the office tonight, Pa,' Taw said. 'I have to ride out to pick up Crow. With him behind bars the business will be as good as over.'

Brenda came scurrying into the doorway of the cell block, her face tense.

'You don't have to ride out to Cadell's place, Taw,' she said swiftly. 'I just heard Crow's voice outside the office. He spoke to Mrs Temple.'

Taw's right hand dropped to his side and his face took on a bleak expression. He pulled Brenda into the cell block.

'Stay in here where you'll be safe,' he said, and walked into the office to face the street door.

He drew his pistol, checked the loads, and then spun the cylinder. The street door opened and the big figure of Barney Crow appeared. Crow blinked against the lamplight, then tensed when he saw Taw's motionless figure.

'My horse went lame so I had to come back to town,' Crow said. 'I thought you'd be dead by now, Landry. Where are those two stupid fools who were supposed to finish you off?'

'Weir is in a cell and Todd is lying dead on the sidewalk near the back of the wagon out there,' Taw replied.

Crow grimaced. 'I saw someone lying out there and thought it was the town drunk. It sure looks like you've been real busy.'

'Whitney is behind bars,' Taw said. 'I found some of the stolen stage office money on him. Now it's your turn, Crow. Throw up your hands and surrender or pull your gun.'

Crow shook his head. He dropped his hand to his gun butt and flexed his fingers. For an interminable moment he gazed at Taw, his eyes narrowed, emotionless. Then his hand moved fast and his pistol seemed to flow out of its holster. Taw moved simultaneously. His gun cleared leather and lifted. The crash of two shots rang out, shaking the office. Taw's bullet smashed into Crow's chest as a sliver of wood sprang out of the desk where Crow's bullet struck.

Crow twisted and fell to the floor. Taw tried to hold his breath against the gun smoke that swirled around him. He suddenly realized that it was all over bar the shouting, and felt empty inside, drained of determination, exhausted by the eternal chasing around. A long sigh escaped him.

Brenda emerged from the cell block, her face showing anxiety, and she clutched at Taw's arm. He holstered his deadly pistol, and told himself there would be better days to follow.

THE END

WARRICK'S BATTLE

Terrell L. Bowers

Haunted by the past, Paul Warrick is assailed by bad memories, and in an attempt to forget, drifts from town to town finding work. But a shoot-out at a casino lands him in jail, and with the valley on the verge of a range war, Paul's actions might be the fire to light the fuse. Paul becomes involved in the final show-down — and he must not only save his life, but also his own sanity at the same time!